Dammit all!

Tim couldn't say ~~what he~~
wanted to say to L~~indsey. I love~~
you. Not yet!

It would shock Lindsey. Right now it
seemed better to let his body speak for him.

He cupped her face, threading his fingertips
into the hair at her temples. Then he
lowered his head.

Lindsey was mesmerized, her eyes wide
open as Tim's face descended, closer,
closer. His mouth touched hers. His lips
were soft and smooth.

The surge of liquid warmth that spread
throughout her body as he went on kissing
her made her involuntarily lift her hands
and grip his shoulders. Her nipples tingled;
desire, heavy and hot, pulsed in her lower
body as she felt his erection pressed
against her.

This is wrong! she thought. *This is Tim.
My younger partner!* She pulled away from
him, breathing hard. "We shouldn't have
done that," she gasped.

"I don't agree," he said roughly. "We should
have done exactly that and more, a long,
long time ago."

Since **Karen Percy** really enjoys reading romances about older women and younger men, she decided to write one for her Temptation fans. Once she had her couple, Lindsey and Tim, clearly in mind, she planned to focus on the problems and insecurities that even a confident woman like Lindsey would have loving a younger man. Then Karen added another interesting complication: the difficult process a man and a woman must go through when they convert friendship to love. When Karen isn't writing terrific Temptations, she is teaching at California State University, and on a free-lance basis, she is a percussionist with the Los Angeles Philharmonic Orchestra.

Books by Karen Percy

HARLEQUIN TEMPTATION
260–THE HOME STRETCH

Don't miss any of our special offers. Write to us at the following address for information on our newest releases.

Harlequin Reader Service
P.O. Box 1397, Buffalo, NY 14240
Canadian address: P.O. Box 603,
Fort Erie, Ont. L2A 5X3

Love Counts

KAREN PERCY

Harlequin Books

TORONTO • NEW YORK • LONDON
AMSTERDAM • PARIS • SYDNEY • HAMBURG
STOCKHOLM • ATHENS • TOKYO • MILAN

Published May 1991

ISBN 0-373-25446-6

LOVE COUNTS

1

LINDSAY AMES watched with amusement as her best friend, Joanne Stephenson, shoved dishes and glassware to the edges of the table. A deck of brightly colored tarot cards lay in the space previously occupied by the remains of Joanne's lunch.

A waiter suddenly appeared beside them and asked nervously, "Would you ladies like me to clear your table?"

Lindsay smiled. "I think you'd better. My friend needs some space."

"Yes, please," Joanne echoed, and the young man hurriedly removed the precariously placed glassware, and plates.

Lindsay hadn't even bothered to protest when Joanne announced that she was going to do a tarot reading for her. Resisting Joanne was generally futile. Lindsay had learned this lesson well during the course of their twenty-five-year-long friendship. Both women's lives had changed—considerably—since they'd met in high school. But it was ironic how similar the direction their lives had taken: marriage, children—she had a daughter; Joanne, two sons—and then divorce. As they approached the big four-O, their friendship was as strong as it had ever been.

As Joanne shuffled the deck, Lindsay heard a murmur from an adjoining table. "Look, Harry! Those women are playing *cards!*"

Lindsay stifled a smile. She had learned to be relatively unfazed by anything Joanne chose to do in public or in private. Still, it sometimes amazed her that they had become friends in the first place. No two women could have been more dissimilar—both in personality and appearance. Lindsay was tall, brunette and slender; Joanne was petite, had a wild mop of curly red hair and constantly battled a tendency to plumpness. Even in high school, Joanne had been the irrepressible kook, ready to try anything new, while Lindsay carefully thought out her plans and goals.

Admittedly, she hadn't planned to be married at nineteen and to have Dina not long thereafter. And no one *planned* on a divorce. But other than that, things had gone pretty much the way they were supposed to. With the accountancy degree she had earned while Dina was in elementary school, she had established a successful practice. She had adjusted—to being divorced and being a single mother. Dina had adjusted, too, and was doing fairly well in her first semester as a freshman at the University of California, Santa Barbara. And thankfully she was less than a two-hour drive up the coast from the Los Angeles suburb where Lindsay had her home and business.

"Oh, shoot!" Joanne suddenly exclaimed, and scooped the cards back into a pile. "I forgot. *You're* supposed to shuffle the deck, or at least touch it, and think very hard of the question you want to ask."

The waiter's shadow crossed the table. "Your check, ladies," he said, then retreated.

Lindsay glanced at her watch. "Well, okay," she agreed reluctantly. "I don't have a lot of time, though. I've got a client coming at one-thirty."

"It won't take a minute," Joanne promised. "And I really need the practice. It's less than two weeks until the benefit."

Despite her novice status as a tarot reader, Joanne had rashly promised to play Madame Mysteria, complete with veils and turban, at a "do" being thrown by one of her pet charities.

Lindsay took the deck and shuffled it.

"Are you thinking of the question you want answered?"

Lindsay frowned. "Give me a minute." She didn't really believe in astrology or tarot cards. Even if she had, she couldn't think of a single thing she wanted to know right now. Oh, she could ask whether she and her partner, Tim Reynolds, would survive tax season. However, she was pretty sure that wasn't the kind of question Joanne had in mind.

Joanne wrinkled her nose. "I swear, Lindsay Ames, you're the only woman I know who wouldn't have the obvious question right on the tip of her tongue. The only *single* woman, anyway."

Lindsay's narrow eyebrows lifted. "The obvious question, then, must be—"

"Am I going to meet Mr. Right soon?" Joanne said promptly. "Say 'In the next two weeks'—the tarot works better if you're specific. Or, 'Someone tall, dark and devastating.'"

"Okay, if that's the sort of thing I'm supposed to ask...."

"It's the sort of thing you ought to *want* to ask," Joanne said emphatically. "I don't know about you, Lindsay. Didn't anyone ever tell you it's possible to be too self-sufficient?"

"Just you."

"I keep thinking one day maybe it'll sink in," Joanne added calmly.

Lindsay hoped it wouldn't. She liked her life the way it was. Friends. A good professional relationship with Tim. And a good relationship with Dina, too. Every now and then, dates with men she knew and liked. No intense emotional upheavals anymore which was just fine with her. Just the way she wanted it. Oh, it might be *nice* to be in love, to meet someone wonderful; but it certainly wasn't essential to her well-being.

"All right. If I must, I must." She curled her fingers around the tarot pack. "Will I meet Mr. Right soon, sometime within the next . . . month?"

"That's better." Joanne took the deck from Lindsay and began to deal.

"AND AFTER ALL THAT," Lindsay finished, "she'd left the book at home that explains the meanings of the various cards, and she could only remember a couple of them, so I didn't get a reading, after all."

Tim Reynolds laughed. He had inquired about Joanne, and Lindsay had told the tale, omitting only the exact nature of the question Joanne had maneuvered her into asking. "Joanne's great," he said. "You never know what she's going to come up with next."

He had a hip perched on the corner of Lindsay's desk so she was looking up at him. As usual, she enjoyed the view. She hadn't asked Tim to be her partner for aesthetic reasons; still, it didn't hurt a bit that he was such a hunk—tall and broad shouldered, with thick chestnut hair.

She found it hard to choose which of his features appealed to her the most. Some days it was his wide, humorous mouth. Other days, it was his smiling eyes that sometimes looked brown, sometimes hazel. Or then again, maybe it was his eyebrows. Except for a few stray hairs in the left one that fanned out across the bridge of his nose, they were well defined, and as he spoke he raised, lowered or arched them to emphasize his points. Lindsay often reflected that even if she went deaf, she would know exactly what Tim was talking about—just from watching his eyebrows.

Now and then, she thought—and the thought was instantly and ruthlessly suppressed—that it was too damn bad about Tim. Too bad that he was ten years younger than she, *and* her partner. Too bad that those were two excellent reasons why she would never find out with her fingertips exactly how muscular were the broad shoulders and wide chest hidden beneath the suits and sports jackets he wore to the office; or how that mobile mouth would feel on hers....

Can it, Lindsay, she told herself firmly as she invariably did when her mind strayed into forbidden territory. She was perfectly satisfied that Tim was what he was to her: her business partner and, more and more, a very good friend.

"I know one thing she's going to come up with next," Lindsay said, responding to Tim's comment about Joanne. "She's going to drag me to that benefit. Evidently it's sort of a fair, with various booths and games."

"What's it for?"

"I forget. You know Joanne and her causes. She has a million of them."

"Actually, it sounds like fun to me. I haven't been to a fair in years."

She looked up at him in mild surprise. It didn't sound like the kind of thing Tim would enjoy. During the eighteen months of their partnership, he had proved to be infinitely surprising. "If you really mean it, I'll give you the information—when and where, and all that. Be forewarned," she teased. "Joanne is bound to insist on doing a tarot reading for you."

"Fine with me. I wouldn't mind a glimpse into the future."

"I already know what's in *my* immediate future—Mr. Sutherland."

A few minutes before, Tim had brought her up-to-date on a recent change in interpretation of the tax law that Mr. Sutherland was bound to quiz her about.

Mr. Sutherland was one of their most persnickety clients. Most clients didn't start making appointments to have their taxes done until they received their W-2s at the end of January. Not Mr. Sutherland. Come mid-January, he would be raring to go, inundating her with his endless lists of dubious tax deductions.

Tim groaned sympathetically. "Tell you what. I'll take him next year."

Lindsay smiled gratefully at him. "Would you really?"

"Sure." He got up off the desk and shrugged. "We're partners, aren't we? Share and share alike—the bitter with the sweet."

"You're a good man, Tim Reynolds," she told him fervently.

He made an "Aw, shucks!" face, his expressive eyebrows dipping in mock embarrassment, then turned to go.

As he reached the door, Lindsay's glance fell on the open desk calendar in front of her. "Oh, Tim," she said as his hand touched the knob, "I just noticed that the Jensons' party is tomorrow night." The Jensons, clients of the firm, threw a bash mid-January every year, claiming that people needed a post-holiday lift. "Are you planning to go?"

He nodded. "As a matter of fact, I meant to ask you if you wanted to ride with me. If you were going by yourself, I mean."

"I was." Without thinking, she added, "Aren't you taking Bambi?" As soon as the words were out, Lindsay wished she could snatch them back. Not that there was anything unusual about her remark. Ever since Tim had become her partner, she'd teased him about his love life—what seemed to be a string of interchangeable blondes, each of whom lasted only a few months before Tim traded her in on a new model. Lindsay had started jokingly referring to all of them, in turn, as "Bambi."

Tim always took her teasing good-naturedly. Even though he was smiling now, Lindsay regretted her waspish remark. It almost sounded as if she were jealous.

That was ridiculous, of course. The fact that her libido recognized what a gorgeous man Tim was had nothing to do with anything.

"Nope," he said easily. "As a matter of fact, I think I'm going to give up on the Bambis for a while."

Lindsay laughed. "I'll believe that when I see it."

"Then get ready to start believing."

Tim's tone was light but firm. He wasn't sure exactly when dissatisfaction with the kind of women he'd been dating had set in. It had been months since he'd cared enough to pursue a "new" Bambi. It was a sign that, at twenty-nine, he was finally growing up, he concluded; becoming too mature for the fleeting satisfactions the

Bambis had once given him, despite the fact that his long stretch of celibacy sometimes got to him.

What he'd really like was to meet a woman his own age who was like Lindsay. The lady really had it together. Not only did he admire her business savvy and her close relationship with her daughter, he liked the fact that she seemed to know exactly who she was and was comfortable with herself. None of the women he'd dated could measure up to Lindsay, or even come close.

She was also an extremely attractive woman. An oval face, delicate features and dark brown hair that shone with vitality and looked smooth as silk, whether it was hanging loose to frame her face and touch the tops of her shoulders, or done up in the French braid she sometimes wore.

No uptight businesswoman suits for her, either. Her look was Southern California casual—dresses that flowed when she moved. Watching her walk, he felt a vague longing, and sometimes a stirring of desire. Feelings that were inappropriate, to say the least.

These feelings embarrassed him a bit, and he was not easily embarrassed. Lindsay had never given a single sign that she ever thought of him as anything but a partner and friend. Obviously those stirrings had to be ignored.

At the moment, she was regarding him quizzically. "Something wrong?" she asked, and he realized he'd been silent for a while.

"Nope. Not a thing. So, what do you think? Shall we team up for the Jensons' bash?"

"If you're sure you want to," Lindsay replied. She wouldn't want to cramp his style, if he should happen to meet someone young and suitable at the Jensons' whose parties tended to be a mix of all ages and types of people.

"I'm sure. Pick you up at seven?"

"OKAY, I DID IT!" Joanne sounded triumphant. The phone had been ringing when Lindsay unlocked the front door of her house. She'd answered it in the kitchen. Now she propped the receiver between her shoulder and ear, leaving her hands free to unpack the groceries she'd stopped off to buy on the way home from the office.

"Did what?" she asked Joanne.

"Did a tarot reading for you."

Lindsay weighed a package of ground beef in her hand. Freeze it? It depended on whether or not Dina decided to come home this weekend from Santa Barbara. Though it might be more convenient at moments like this if she asked Dina to always let her know her plans, it was more important to Lindsay that her daughter feel free to appear any time she chose. This was still her home, after all, even if she was away at college.

To Joanne, she said, "I thought I had to be there, thinking about my question, while you laid out the cards."

"We-ell," Joanne answered uncertainly, "it's better that way. But I'm pretty sure it works any way. I'll have to ask my instructor about that." She paused, then said eagerly, "Don't you want to hear?"

"Sure," Lindsay replied, injecting some enthusiasm into her tone. "I mean, of course I do, Joanne." Freeze the hamburger, she decided. If Dina did show up later tonight or tomorrow morning, she could always thaw it again. Or they could go out for pizza before the Jensons' party.

And then she registered what Joanne was saying. "Three times," her friend's excited voice repeated. "Three times I laid out the cards and each time it was the same. You're definitely going to meet Mr. Right, Lindsay. Soon. Within the next few weeks."

"Am I?" Lindsay stifled a chuckle. "That's nice to know. Maybe I should buy something new to wear, just in case."

"I would if I were you," Joanne told her seriously.

"Is he going to be tall, dark and handsome?"

"Well, naturally. Or he wouldn't *be* Mr. Right. He's definitely dark. The King of Swords kept turning up, and that means a dark man. There's no actual way to know about his height from the cards though."

"Then he could be a dark, handsome midget," Lindsay joked.

"Honestly!" Joanne sounded offended. "You're not taking any of this seriously, are you?"

"Nope," Lindsay said cheerfully.

"You'll see, Lindsay Ames. Mark my words. When you actually meet him, you'll be sorry you scoffed."

"I'll gladly eat crow if it happens."

"Not crow," Joanne corrected decisively. "Something much more delicious. If you do meet Mr. Right within the next month, I'm going to expect a lavish lunch at the restaurant of my choice."

"It's a deal." Joanne's choice of restaurant would be madly extravagant, but Lindsay figured she was safe. The odds of her actually meeting someone right for her were small. Weren't there statistics to prove that the chances of a woman of her age remarrying were less than those of her winning a lottery?

"No cheating, now," Joanne warned. "You have to promise to tell me if you meet someone."

If she did, then she'd *want* to tell. She remembered that about being in love—the urge to speak the loved one's name, to drop it into conversations, given the slightest excuse. "I promise. But don't hold your breath."

"Humpf! You'll see! Now, tell me, what are your plans for the weekend?"

"Nothing in particular. Oh, tomorrow night, I'm going to a client's party."

"Well, you see? You might even meet Mr. Right there."

LINDSAY DID A last-minute inventory in front of the bathroom mirror. Hair, up in a French braid—check. Makeup, not too much or too little—check. Little black dress, flattering to her figure, yet cut discreetly enough to be appropriate to a woman CPA meeting potential clients—also check. She paused a moment over the glittery earrings dangling from her ears. Too much? Nope. Properly festive for a post-holiday party.

She grabbed a wrap from the hall closet when she heard Tim's car pull up out front. She was halfway down the walk by the time he'd opened the driver's-side door. "Stay where you are," she called. "I'm coming."

But Tim stepped out onto the street. He looked striking—no, make that stunning, Lindsay corrected herself—in a dark gray suit that hinted at the currently fashionable shape without being overly trendy.

"Oh, come on, Lindsay," he complained with a grin. "You've got to let me play gentleman or I'll get out of practice." He hurried around the low-slung silvery car to open the door for her.

"Thank you, kind sir." Lindsay sat down, then reached for her seat belt while Tim walked back around to the driver's side. She tugged on the buckle but couldn't make the belt snake out more than a few inches. As Tim got in and closed his door, she said, "There's something wrong with this thing."

"Shoot!" Tim responded disgustedly. "That's been happening on and off for weeks. I've taken it in twice to get it fixed. At the garage, it worked fine, naturally. Let me see if I can do it."

He leaned across her, his wrist brushing her shoulder as he grasped the buckle. When his hand briefly touched her arm, Lindsay felt a familiar tingling sensation. Suddenly, she was overwhelmingly aware of the warmth of his body, and of his scent—a clean, salt smell, mixed with a hint of spicy after-shave.

Down, girl! There was nothing new about this response. If anything, it was annoyingly predictable. She had been close to Tim before, at the office, and it was always the same. If he happened to touch her, no matter how casually and briefly, there was always that mildly intoxicating rush of sensation. That was just because her body was a dumb animal. It simply couldn't get it figured out that Tim was off-limits.

She pressed herself against the seat back, out of the way, as Tim pulled the seat belt free. "There we go," he said. His voice sounded strange. Tense, maybe. As if something was bothering him.

Tim started to snap the buckle into place at Lindsay's hip. He changed his mind and handed the end of the seat belt over to her instead. Maybe he should find himself a new girlfriend, after all. His months of celibacy must be having an effect. There had been no vague stirrings in *that* brief moment of contact with Lindsay, but rather a powerful erotic surge—and an intense desire to lean over a little farther, cup her face in his hands and kiss her.

Wrong! All wrong, Tim, my boy! Doing something like that would violate the unspoken canons of their relationship, threatening their friendship and business association. Besides, Lindsay would doubtless think he'd gone berserk.

He turned the key in the ignition. "Let's see," he said lightly. "Are there any potential clients we're trying to impress tonight?"

"No one in particular. We should do some circulating, of course. Basically, we can just relax and enjoy ourselves."

Yes, relax, Tim echoed mentally. There was still tension in his groin from that brief moment of being so close to Lindsay.

It would be a darn good thing, Lindsay thought as she glanced over at Tim, if Joanne's tarot cards turned out to be right and a suitable male did turn up in her life. The fact that her body kept on reacting to Tim the way it did must be a sign that her subconscious was clamoring for a little love life.

A SMILING, slightly rotund Roland Jenson opened the door and they were propelled into a party that was already in full swing. Their host introduced them to other guests.

For the next hour, sipping a single drink, Lindsay conversed with various people. Being naturally sociable, she was soon having a pleasant time.

When she began feeling hungry, she excused herself from her current circle to head over to the lavishly stocked buffet table set up at one end of the living room, and selected a roast-beef sandwich. As she swallowed the last of it a young woman with blond hair cut short in the latest style sidled up to her. "Nice party, isn't it?" she commented.

"Very nice," Lindsay agreed.

"I don't really know the Jensons very well," she confided. "They're friends of my dad. They seem like nice people."

"Yes, they are," Lindsay said.

"I noticed you when you came in. Your date's really a great-looking guy."

At last the girl had gotten to her reason for making conversation. "He's not really my date. We're business partners."

She smiled. "I wondered about that. He seemed, uh—"

"Younger than me," Lindsay cut in. "Ten years, roughly. He's not attached to anybody at the moment," she added, anticipating the girl's next question. She gestured across the room to where Tim was standing with a couple of suited businessmen types and their wives. "Go for it!"

"Gee, that's great. Thanks! I'll let you know how I make out."

Spare me, Lindsay thought as she watched as the girl steered an oblique course in Tim's direction.

For the next several minutes, Lindsay observed the blonde's approach. She had to give the girl points for technique. A nice job of casual lurking on the fringes of the group that included Tim. Clever insinuation of herself into the circle. An A + for the neat maneuver that drew Tim apart from the others.

A man who had been standing near the buffet table turned toward Lindsay and smiled. "Hello. We haven't met, have we?" He transferred his plate to his left hand and extended his right. "I'm Adam Holloway."

Lindsay slid her hand into his. He was nice looking. In his late forties, maybe, with sandy-brown hair graying at the temples. "Lindsay Ames."

"Nice to meet you, Lindsay." Releasing her hand, he said in mock-confidential tones, "I'm the Jensons' dentist. Don't tell anyone, okay?"

"It's a secret?"

"At parties, it is. If no one knows, then I won't have to peer at anyone's fillings."

Lindsay laughed. "I know exactly what you mean."

"You don't mean you're a dentist, too?"

She shook her head. "A CPA. The price I pay is having to give free tax advice. Not as bad as having to stare into someone's mouth, I'll admit, but not a whole lot of fun, either."

"So we have something in common, don't we, Lindsay?" He looked around the room, winked and bluntly asked, "Is your husband here?"

"No husband," Lindsay replied. "I'm divorced."

His grin widened. "Aha! One more thing we have in common. Let's see what else we can come up with."

TIM WAS GETTING BORED, and slightly irritated with the Bambi who absolutely wouldn't leave him alone. The girl—Jennifer—had attached herself to him like a limpet. He hadn't seen Lindsay in ages. Jennifer had been regaling him with enthusiastic descriptions of her favorite rock-and-roll clubs—an exercise designed, no doubt, to suggest that he might take her to one of them.

"Well, it's been nice talking to you. I think I'd better get going."

Jennifer pouted. "Oh, you're not leaving so *soon!*"

"'Fraid so. My partner mentioned that she didn't want to stay too late." Lindsay had never said any such thing.

"Oh, her? That dark-haired lady? I think she left already."

"*What?* She wouldn't have done that without telling me." He brushed past the girl, then was sorry that he'd hurt her feelings. Still, she was exactly the kind of woman he had vowed not to get involved with anymore.

Tim glanced around the living room. No Lindsay. He scowled. She wouldn't have just left; he was certain of it. Lindsay was always polite. More than polite. She was genuinely kind. He witnessed it daily in her dealings with their office staff.

Then he noticed an open door. He walked over to it and looked inside. The room was a huge family room, with a TV and bookshelves and several couches. He heard Lindsay's laugh and zeroed in on the sound, spotting her in a dim corner, seated in an easy chair. In an adjacent wing chair was a distinguished-looking older man. From the way he and Lindsay were smiling at each other, it looked as if they were having a very good time. *Too* good a time.

Irrationally angry, Tim gritted his teeth. Here he'd been, fending off a Bambi, and Lindsay had had the nerve to be enjoying herself.

"There you are," he said. "I've been looking for you."

Lindsay looked up. Tim had his feathers ruffled about something, she saw at once. The way his eyebrows were flattened down was a dead giveaway.

"Ready to go?" she asked. Obviously, the girl who had accosted her at the buffet table had struck out. Maybe Tim really was giving up on the Bambi types.

Tim nodded brusquely. "If you are."

"Sure." She rose. "Adam, I'd like you to meet my partner, Tim Reynolds. Tim, Adam Holloway."

Adam stood, acknowledging the introduction. The two men shook hands and exchanged small talk for a few moments.

Then Adam turned to Lindsay. "I'll give you a call around Wednesday, if that's okay, and we'll firm up our plans."

Plans? Tim could almost feel his ears pricking up. She'd been making *plans* with this guy she'd just met? What kind of plans?

It took several minutes after their departure before he had mastered himself enough to say grudgingly to Lindsay, "Sorry. I didn't mean to interrupt anything in there."

They were walking down the dark suburban street to where Tim had parked his car. "You didn't," Lindsay replied. "Don't worry about it." Before Tim had come in, she'd already agreed to go out with Adam Holloway next weekend. Adam wasn't dark, so he didn't exactly fit the description given by Joanne's tarot cards. But he seemed nice. In fact, there was no reason in the world he couldn't turn out to be the quasimythical Mr. Right. She ought to be excited about the date with him. Maybe she'd feel a little more excitement as the day approached.

She glanced at Tim. He seemed uptight about something. "Have a good time?" she asked.

With an abruptness that struck Lindsay as being extremely unlike him, he said, "No."

2

Tim awoke groggily and winced as he opened an eye. Since he never drank when he was driving, he'd drunk only cola at the Jensons' party. When he'd reached home, he'd been in a perverse mood and had slugged down a double Scotch—maybe two double Scotches, come to think of it.

He flinched as he cautiously rolled out of bed. His mouth felt as if it were lined with a fuzzy woollen blanket and his stomach . . . He wouldn't think about his stomach.

That wasn't the only subject he was deliberately avoiding. There was also the memory of a revelation that had struck him after his first double Scotch, sending him for a second one.

He held the revelation at bay as he pulled on a short brown terry-cloth robe and made his way to the kitchen. He grimaced when he saw the Scotch bottle sitting on the Formica counter. Deliberately gotten drunk, that was what he'd done. And he thought he'd long ago put such juvenile behavior behind him.

As he filled the coffeepot with water, he realized that something other than the state of his head was different this morning from his usual wakenings of late: it was quiet.

Across from his condo, on the uphill side of the street, they were tearing down a row of older homes to make way for another condominium complex—a much larger one than the small two-story stucco building where he lived. Soon the whole street would be nothing but condos and apartment complexes; the quiet residential charm that had attracted him to this neighborhood would be gone forever.

So it was a small blessing that today was Sunday. No bulldozers dozing; no dump trucks roaring past, carrying loads of debris. There was rain forecast for the coming week, he recalled, which might mean a temporary reprieve for the remaining small houses. But soon the last one would go and construction, with *its* attendant noises, would begin.

He leaned against the counter, watching the coffee drip into the glass container, and knew he could no longer put off acknowledging the reason he'd acted like such a jerk at the end of the Jensons' party and while taking Lindsay home.

He'd been jealous.

Over Lindsay.

It was seeing her so cozy and intimate with that dentist guy that had done it—and then discovering that the tooth puller had evidently asked her out and she'd accepted. It appalled him how much he hated the idea of Lindsay going out with that guy or, if he was honest with himself, with anyone.

He poured himself a cup of coffee and took it to the living room. The view through his front window was of a partly rubbled lot and the noses of trucks and dozers on the intersecting side street where the crew parked the heavy equipment when it wasn't in use. Charming, he thought ironically.

Irritably, he pulled the drapes shut, darkening the room, and sat down in his favorite reclining chair. His head was a little better. After a while, he'd rouse himself and take a couple of aspirins. First, he'd better get a handle on this jealousy nonsense.

It wouldn't do. That was clear. The occasional twinges of desire he felt for Lindsay were one thing. Those, he could deal with. But he simply couldn't let himself get all hot and bothered about her.

Jealous, for God's sake! As if he had some claim on her, other than the bonds of friendship and partnership. It was no business of his whom she dated. A true friend—which he liked to think he was—would be glad to see her happy.

Yet the thought of that Adam guy being the source of her happiness made his stomach churn, and he was pretty certain it had nothing to do with the Scotch he'd consumed the night before.

He plainly had to put a stop to those feelings. Lindsay wouldn't appreciate them. If she knew—and pray to heaven she never would—there was too much to lose.

Office romances were notoriously dangerous. Their situation was even worse. They had a first-class working partnership. If he made a move on her and she rejected him, it would be damnably awkward, probably for a long, long time thereafter. And if, by chance, she *didn't* reject him—which he didn't have much hope of happening—and *then* things went wrong between them, it could mean the loss of everything.

He was starting to feel like a jerk, sitting in a dark room, tormenting himself over a woman he couldn't have. He swallowed the last of the tepid coffee in his cup, went to the window and opened the drapes. It had started to rain, which made the half-demolished site across the way look even bleaker.

Enough! He left the living room, first to take some aspirin, then to call a friend he played racquetball with sometimes. That was what he needed—physical activity to sweat last night's poisons out of his system and distract him from all those fruitless thoughts of Lindsay Ames.

"TIM IN YET, Nancy?" Lindsay paused at their secretary-receptionist's desk first thing Monday morning.

Nancy Buttrick, a woman of determination who refused to give in gracefully to the ravages of time, was past sixty. Her hair was a brassy shade of blonde not found on Mother Nature's palette, her figure slim by virtue of dieting and exercise, and her clothing ultra up-to-date. Nancy was a treasure, as far as Lindsay was concerned. Pleasant with the clients. Incredibly efficient. All the virtues wrapped up in a slightly gaudy package.

"Yep," Nancy said. "He's been here for a while, going over his first client's file, I think."

"Thanks." It was a tradition for Lindsay and Tim to chat for a few minutes each morning. Once a week they also met with their five-member staff of bookkeepers and accountants. Lindsay took a couple of steps past Nancy's desk, then paused and turned back. "What kind of mood is he in this morning?"

Nancy swiveled around in her chair to stare at Lindsay. "Mood? Tim? That man doesn't have moods. You know that as well as I do." Her carefully penciled eyebrows nearly met above the bridge of her nose. "He's always 'up,' as far as I can tell."

"I know," Lindsay agreed. "it's just that he was a little grumpy the other night after the Jensons' party."

"Well, he's fine now. Big smile, as usual." Nancy grinned fondly. "That man's smile. I swear." The phone on her desk rang and she turned back to answer it. "Ames and Reynolds," she said briskly while Lindsay went on into the hallway. To the right were her office and Tim's; to the left, the rooms where their employees worked.

She tapped on his door, heard him call "Come in," and entered. *That man's smile!* It wasn't just a matter of white teeth and curving lips. It was the way his whole face lit up.

"Morning, partner," she said cheerily. "Ready for a little conferring?"

"Sure."

She took a seat in the easy chair, hoisting her briefcase onto his desk. She looked over at him. The smile was gone; his face was somber, his eyebrows dead level. Had Nancy been wrong? Was he still in a bad mood? Moodiness wasn't Tim's style. She hoped there was nothing wrong in his personal life or with his family back in the Midwest.

She toyed with the latches of her briefcase for a moment. In the eighteen months she and Tim had worked together, they'd learned quite a lot about each other's lives and backgrounds. Nevertheless, they'd never gotten into the habit of exchanging deeply personal confidences. It was best that way because it helped preserve the integrity of their professional relationship.

Lindsay wondered if she should ask Tim if something was bothering him, or whether that might be construed as prying. Then again he *was* her friend. She looked closely at him and began, "Tim, is something—"

At the same moment, he said, "Lindsay, I—"

They both laughed, though Lindsay noticed that Tim's laugh wasn't as robust as usual. He waved his hand. "Ladies first."

"No. You go ahead."

He nodded. A memo pad with a list of topics for this morning's discussion lay on the desk in front of him. He kept his eyes on it as he said "Lindsay, I want to apologize."

Her eyes widened in surprise. "Apologize? For what?"

"For the way I acted Saturday night. I was behaving like a real jerk and I'm sorry."

Her smile was wide and genuine. "No, you weren't. Not really, Tim. You were a little . . . silent. Maybe just a teeny bit cross. But you certainly weren't a jerk."

"Well, I felt like one. And I'm really sorry about it."

"No need. None at all," she stated firmly, then paused before adding, "I did wonder if something was bothering you."

He gave a quick shake of his head. "Nothing important. I've got it straightened out now."

That was true—he hoped. A tiring afternoon of racquetball and a good night's sleep had restored his perspective. He couldn't dismiss that attack of jealousy he'd felt over the idea of Lindsay being with some other man. It had been real enough. No doubt about that. Yet he *could* ignore it, push it down and keep it there, refuse to think about her in those terms.

He looked at her now, testing his ability to regard her purely as friend and partner. Her dark hair was swept back from the sides of her face, secured by a tortoiseshell clip at the nape of her neck. Her makeup was light, subtle—the way she always wore it. Her full-skirted suit was a russet color. He was pleased with himself that he could notice those things about her without feeling the slightest stirring of desire. He was getting this thing well under control. It wasn't going to turn out to be a problem, after all.

But then she gave a little laugh. "It's warm in here, isn't it? I'll have to tell Nancy not to turn the thermostat quite so high."

As she spoke, she slipped her arms out of the russet suit-jacket and let it fall over the back of the chair. Tim's mouth went dry. Underneath the loose-fitting jacket, she was wearing a long-sleeved, high-necked white silk blouse that clung to her torso. He noticed that she was slender, her breasts were full and round. And since she had borne a child, the nipples would be . . .

He had no business thinking about Lindsay's nipples, feeling a surge of anger at himself. Along with the dryness in his mouth, he now had a dull ache in his groin. He was more than half erect. If he had to rise from behind his desk, she'd see.

"Tim," she prompted. "We'd better get started. I have a nine o'clock appointment."

"Me, too," he said hastily. So much for how well he was doing, fighting down his feelings for Lindsay. Well, he thought grimly, he'd have to try harder.

He looked down at the list in front of him, forcing the words into focus. "The first thing we should talk about," he began, "is the Forrester audit."

As they discussed the situation, Lindsay answered mechanically. Something about the way Tim had been looking at her . . .

He'd said that whatever had been bothering him Saturday night was both unimportant and over. Yet he still seemed bothered—by something. Obviously, he didn't want to tell her about it, so she wouldn't ask. She decided to keep an eye on him—not that *that* would be much of a chore—during the next few days and weeks. She cared for Tim and wanted him to be happy.

She remembered the first time they'd met. He'd been starting out on his own as a CPA and one of his clients was the soon-to-be ex-wife of one of Lindsay's regulars. The four of them had met to try to iron out a knotty tax problem that was plaguing the divorcing couple. The meeting had degenerated into sniping shots fired between the warring pair when Mrs. What's-It griped that her husband had taken *all* the place mats when he moved out, Lindsay's eyes and Tim's had met. His eyebrows had lifted and fallen in a commentary that had forced Lindsay to stare very hard at the conference table to keep from bursting into laughter.

Later in the meeting, Tim had made a particularly astute suggestion for the handling of the What's-Its' financial problems—something Lindsay never would have thought of herself.

Several months before, she had decided it would be wise for her to take on a partner—if she could only find the right person. By the time that conference had ended, she was reasonably certain that Tim Reynolds was the partner she'd been looking for.

Three more meetings with Tim had only confirmed her initial impression. She had asked if he was interested and he had swiftly agreed. Since then, not for one minute had she regretted it.

Tim's voice snapped her back to the present. "Okay, I think that does it."

"Oh . . . right," Lindsay faltered. She glanced at her watch. Almost nine. Her first client, the ever-prompt owner of a small business whose books they kept, was probably in the reception area already.

She closed her briefcase and rose, then took her jacket from the back of the chair and draped it over her arm. She said quietly, "I may be out of line saying this, Tim, but if ever something *is* bothering you—like whatever it was on Saturday night—well, I just want you to know that if you need someone to talk to—" her laugh was slightly embarrassed "—I'm available for consultation. Okay?"

Tim held himself still. "Thank you, Lindsay. I appreciate that."

She picked up her briefcase and walked to the door. He deliberately *didn't* watch her.

"Okay. See you later, then," she said.

"See you later," he echoed. He groaned as the door closed behind her. Talk to Lindsay about what was bothering him? She was the last person in the world he could confide in.

"THE HATCHES ARE battened," Tim announced. He stood just inside the door of Lindsay's office. It was late Friday afternoon, and only the weekend stood between Ames and Reynolds, CPAs, and the real beginning of the tax-season onslaught. Everyone in the office, especially Lindsay and Tim, had been working like mad to ensure that all their other work was up-to-date.

Lindsay leaned forward and rested her elbows on her desk. "Are you sure?"

"As sure as I can be." His eyebrows did a little dance. "Now that I've said that, there are bound to be a dozen loose ends I've overlooked."

Lindsay smiled. "I doubt it. If there are, we'll deal with them."

He grinned, walked over and sat on the arm of one of the visitors' chairs. Ever since Monday, the day he'd apologized to her, Lindsay had been watching, noticing. Little by little, his usual high spirits seemed to have been restored.

He crossed his arms. "You'll never guess who my first client is on Monday—a truly fitting inauguration of the tax season."

"Who?"

"Mr. Goodall."

Lindsay frowned. "I remember the name, but . . ."

"The cardboard-carton king."

Lindsay moaned sympathetically. Tim had told her about Gregory Goodall's visit last year. The man's idea of preparing to have his taxes done was to dump all his receipts and canceled checks into a grocery-store carton and hand the whole thing over to Tim. The firm charged Mr. Goodall plenty, of course. Still . . .

Tim's eyebrows twitched in amusement. "I wonder if it'll be cat litter this year or something else."

"What? Cat litter?"

"The carton. That was what last year's box originally contained. Remember when he came in to pick up his tax return, he wanted the carton back. I told him we'd thrown it out, and he was very indignant. Not indignant enough to go to another accountant, evidently. I can't wait to see if it's cat litter again this year, or something else."

Lindsay chuckled. "Promise to let me know as soon as you can."

"I'll ask Nancy to take you a note. I'm afraid I can't pick up the phone while he's sitting there and mutter 'Toilet paper' or whatever it turns out to be."

"Certainly not!" Lindsay said with a straight face. "We wouldn't want to hurt Mr. Goodall's feelings."

"Unless he was hurt enough to find another accountant," Tim added hopefully.

Lindsay looked serious. "If you don't want to deal with him, Tim, you don't have to. I could take him this year . . . or you could tell him we're too busy."

"No, I really don't mind. I enjoy the eccentrics every now and then. If every client was like Mr. Goodall, though . . . Say, Lindsay, I've been thinking about maybe doing a little something for the staff on Monday morning—a sort of kickoff to the tax season. Nothing too fancy. Maybe just bagels and stuff first thing in the morning, before the clients start coming in. I thought I'd better check with you, first."

"That's a nice idea, Tim. I should have thought of it myself. I'll chip in, of course. If you want me to pick up the food, there's a good deli near my place."

"No need. I'll take care of it." He smiled. "I thought of champagne, but that's not a great idea, I guess."

"No, we don't want everyone getting tipsy just in time to greet the clients." She looked at him quizzically. "You're in an awfully good mood this afternoon."

Tim didn't consider himself to be in a particularly good mood. For the first couple of days after the Jensons' party, it had taken considerable effort to get his thoughts and feelings about Lindsay back on the right track, but he'd done it.

Still, it was a little difficult, with the weekend upon them, for Tim to forget that she'd made a date with the tooth puller.

As if she'd read his mind, she asked, "Any special plans for the weekend?"

Maybe he'd met someone new and that was why he seemed so ebullient.

"Not really. At one point I thought maybe I'd go away somewhere this weekend. I decided to stay home and enjoy the peace and quiet. It'll be the last I'll get for a while. You remember I told you about the construction going on across the way from my place? Well, they've finished knocking down the old houses and leveling out the lot. By Monday morning, it looks like the cement trucks will be coming in." He made a grinding noise. "That's what I'll have to look forward to for the next few months."

"That's too bad," Lindsay said.

He shrugged. "I'll live. How about you? You doing anything exciting this weekend?"

She shot him an acute glance. His voice had sounded slightly strained. Unable to imagine why, she chalked it up to imagination. "Dina's probably coming home tomorrow morning. She called yesterday and said she thought she would."

"That's nice," Tim responded. "Tell her hi for me. She still doing okay in school?"

"Her grades are fine, if that's what you mean, but—"

"Problems?"

Lindsay gave a little shake of her head. "I'm not sure. She sounded kind of down when we talked on the phone. I'm hoping this weekend I'll have a chance to find out what's bugging her."

"I'm sure you will. You two have a really good relationship, don't you? At least, it's always seemed that way to me."

"Not bad for mother and daughter. Somehow we weathered the worst of her teen years without too many storms."

Tim leaned slightly forward, his arms still crossed. His tone was extremely casual. "So that's it for your weekend? You and Dina doing mother-daughter stuff?"

"That's it," Lindsay replied. The moment the words were out, she realized she'd lied; her date with Adam Holloway was scheduled for the following night. But it wasn't worth retracting her original statement, because Tim was already speaking.

Tim felt as if a thousand-pound weight he hadn't known he was carrying had suddenly been lifted from his back. Something must have gone wrong regarding her date with the tooth puller. He felt happy; he felt like celebrating. His mouth opened and words came out: "Well, in that case, I have an idea. Since you're free tonight, and I'm free, why don't we grab a bite of dinner? I could go for some Thai food. Or if you don't feel like Thai, there's a great Italian place on Vanowen. It's more or less on the way home for both of us."

Once he'd heard himself speak, he decided that suggesting dinner was the perfect thing to do. The answer to any remaining Lindsay problem was to become even better friends with her; eliminate any possible mystique; turn her into "good old Lindsay," just another pal.

Good old Lindsay? Do you really think that's going to work? Besides, that's not why you invited her to dinner and you know it! Who did he think he was fooling?

As she took in Tim's invitation, Lindsay's eyes rounded in surprise. She and Tim had working lunches where they hashed out a client's problems while they ate. But he'd never suggested dinner before. It wasn't part of the pattern of their friendship. The break in the familiar pattern made her hesitate.

She looked up to find Tim's eyes on her and a suggestion of tension in his face as he waited for her reply. "Sure, Tim. Why not?" she said lightly.

Why not, indeed? She knew why not. Because there was a bubble of excitement forming inside her, making it hard for her to breathe. It was wrong, all wrong, that she should feel this sense of heady anticipation over dinner with her partner, a man ten years younger than herself, and not over a full-fledged date with the apparently eligible Adam Holloway.

The Smile lit up his face, adding to Lindsay's difficulty with her lungs. "Great," he replied. "Half an hour?"

Lindsay swallowed. "Half an hour's fine."

3

IT WAS TOO EARLY for a crowd at Antonelli's; Lindsay and Tim were alone in the row of booths that stretched along one wall. On the drive there Lindsay had mentally applied sharp-pointed objects to the balloon of her excitement. It was no big deal. Just dinner with her partner.

Now she looked across the table. It was just Tim. He hadn't changed. The few wayward hairs in his left eyebrow still fanned toward the right. His jaw and chin still had the same firm lines, his mouth the same humorous quirk. She had sat across plenty of tables from him during the past year and a half—conference tables, coffee-shop tables, even her own dining-room table at Thanksgiving when he had joined them because his own family was all back in the Midwest. Just because they were in a restaurant for an evening meal shouldn't make this occasion feel so . . . different.

"What's the matter? Do I have a smudge on my nose or something?"

Tim grinned as he spoke and Lindsay realized she'd been staring. She hastily dropped her gaze to the square of white tablecloth framed by her silverware, returning it just as quickly to his face. "No. No smudges," she said lightly, then rushed on: "I hope you really don't mind Italian instead of Thai. I have to admit I'm not crazy about Thai food. I can't handle the blowtorch effect."

Aha! Tim thought. The first actual flaw he'd found in Lindsay. Not liking Thai food was hardly a character defect, though. "Italian's fine. This place is great. The linguine *marinara* is terrific. So's the spaghetti *carbonara*."

A faint smile curved the corners of Lindsay's mouth. "True, but my favorite's the veal *piccata*."

Tim stared at her. She hadn't even opened the menu. "You've been here before," he said accusingly.

"Lots," she told him, then added gently, "Tim, I've lived in this neighborhood for nearly twenty years." It was really only seventeen, but she saw no harm in rounding it off upward.

Tim swallowed his embarrassment. Twenty years, she'd said. And he knew she'd been an adult when she moved to the Los Angeles area. Twenty years ago, he'd been in fourth grade. Normally he didn't think about Lindsay being older. He acknowledged it factually, of course—women *his* age didn't have daughters in college—but the age gap had never seemed to mean anything in particular.

He seized on the reminder as a good thing to point out to his libido. The trouble was, he couldn't seem to make her age have any significance. In the dim, candlelit restaurant, she looked like a girl. Even outdoors in harsh sunlight, there was only a faint line on her forehead, one or two on her throat. Her jawline was tautly delicate, her skin as dewy as a teenager's.

So far, the dinner wasn't working out as he'd hoped. It was supposed to help cement his *friendship* with Lindsay, not make him think of the skin her clothing concealed. He had to blink his eyes to clear away an intoxicating vision of Lindsay's body—slim and lithe, with her full breasts and a dark triangle of hair between her thighs.

He leaned closer, resting his forearms on the table. "Well, you caught me showing off. Demonstrating my familiarity with the menu." His laugh was self-deprecating. "It's supposed to make me look all suave and man-of-the-world-ish, I guess. But it's really just like a little kid." He pitched his voice in a higher register and boasted, "'I've been to Disneyland *three* times!'" And in a slightly different voice, retorted, "'I've been there *four!*'"

Lindsay laughed.

"It's a vice we men have," Tim explained in his own baritone. "Wanting to make it look as if we've been around."

It was true, but she couldn't recall a man actually having admitted it before. That Tim could be so honest about himself was . . . endearing. She was suddenly seized by a desire to lean forward and take his face between her hands, look deeply into his eyes, and assure him that it was okay, that he didn't have to be perfect.

Instead she sat back, pressing her spine against the padded booth. "Women do it, too, sometimes. Besides, it's not a sin. Not a deadly one, anyway."

He swiped imaginary sweat from his brow. "Whew!" Then one side of his mouth lifted in a lopsided smile. "It's still kind of dumb. Almost as bad as the story I used to tell in college—"

He broke off as the waiter approached with his order pad. Nodding his head in Lindsay's direction, Tim said, "The lady's going to order for us both. She's more familiar with the menu than I."

A peal of laughter burst out of Lindsay at the unexpected role reversal. The waiter turned obediently toward her. "Good grief! I never realized what a responsibility it was." She shot an amused glance at Tim. "And you men have to deal with it all the time."

"Just a taste of how the other half lives," he told her smugly.

She ordered, watching Tim's face as she selected a pasta dish for him, since she was pretty sure his eyebrows would give him away if it was something he actually loathed. Then she ordered for herself.

It wasn't until after the waiter had returned to pour a glass of wine for each of them that she said, "You were saying something about a story you told in college."

"Ah, yes, another dumb thing." He chuckled. "It has to do with why I decided to become an accountant."

"Why did you, Tim? I don't think I ever asked you."

"The truth is, I've always been fascinated by numbers. And by the orderliness of accounting. The symmetry of it all, I guess."

Lindsay nodded, feeling much the same.

"When I was in college, I'd try to explain to someone why I was doing what I was doing and they'd look at me as if I were a creature from another planet...or even worse, a dull stick with no life in him." He shrugged. "So after a while, I made up a story."

"A story? About why you wanted to go into accounting? This, I've got to hear."

He twirled an imaginary mustache. "It was a pretty good story, if I do say so myself. It had a villain and a helpless female—my fictional Great-Aunt Lucy."

"Let me guess," Lindsay interjected. "Who was fleeced by an unscrupulous accountant."

"Nope. That version was tempting, but a little too obvious. *My* Great-Aunt Lucy frittered her money away because she had no one to manage it for her."

"Very sad," Lindsay said dryly.

"Oh, very," Tim agreed. "Her fate varied a little, depending on who I was talking to. Sometimes, she ended up living on welfare. Other times, I'd turn her into a bag lady." He laughed. "My parents hated that one when I told them. They said no relative of theirs, real or imaginary, would ever sink that low. Anyway, that was my great college lie. Pretty dumb, huh?"

"Oh, I don't know. Pretty creative, I'd call it."

Their meals arrived and he told more tales of his college days and of growing up in a small Midwestern town. Lindsay was in stitches, as much from the way Tim told his stories as from the stories themselves. It seemed as if he were putting himself out to be especially charming.

Only that wasn't quite right. Tim was always charming. It was that this evening, their conversation didn't need to center around business, as it usually did. Tonight Tim was relaxed and witty.

It must be the way he acted on a date. At that thought, a chill of dismay snaked down her spine. Tim wasn't the only one. She too was acting as if she were on a date—a date with a man who interested and excited her. It was hard to pinpoint the exact difference from the way she usually behaved with Tim, but it definitely *was* different.

At the end of an evening like this one, she would expect to be taken home and kissed good-night. Bone-rattlingly, knee-weakeningly kissed.

That was *not* how this evening was going to end. Not when her companion was Tim. Her partner. That meant she'd better put an end to it before she made a complete fool of herself with any more too-warm glances or too-delighted laughs.

She lifted her arm and stared ostentatiously at her plain gold watch. "Good heavens! Look at the time! I'd better get going."

A look of disappointment crossed Tim's face. He nodded and reached for the check. Lindsay opened her purse. "What's the total?" she asked. "I figure it'll come out about right if we split it fifty-fifty—if that's okay with you."

"My treat."

"Oh, no," Lindsay protested. "I insist on paying my share." At least she could do that much to indicate she didn't *really* think this was a date.

Tim looked at her face, nodding reluctantly. There was a determined cast to her features that told him she'd fight to the bitter end on this one.

He accepted her money. After paying the bill, they walked outside to the parking lot. The sky was clear. The rain had stopped and stars competed valiantly with the lights of the suburban neighborhood. Tim smiled down at her. "It was fun, Lindsay. We'll have to do it again soon."

Again? She wasn't sure she could survive another evening like this—certainly not anytime in the near future.

As they approached her car, he put his arm around her shoulders and gave her a brief hug. Nothing to it, really. He'd hugged her lots of times before, in moments of camaraderie. This time was different. The outline of his ribs brushed the side of her breast; his hip and the long, smoothly muscled length of his thigh pressed against her. Her whole left side felt as if it had come close to an inferno.

Abruptly she pulled away from him, and her voice was high-pitched as she said, "Well, good night, Tim. See you Monday."

TIM DROVE TOWARD his condo. He'd had a wonderful time, and he was pretty sure Lindsay had enjoyed herself, too. It had been a special evening, full of sparks and hints of promise.

He couldn't seem to stop thinking of Lindsay as a potential lover, rather than as a friend and partner.

That hug had been a big mistake. Feeling her body close against his side, he had wanted to pull her around so that she was facing him, wrap his other arm around her and kiss her so deeply and intensely that they would have to cling to each other to stay upright.

He steered his car around the corner, onto his own street. Moon and starlight shone down on the heavy vehicles parked around the construction site, making them look like monsters of the Mesozoic era.

After the hug had been in some ways even worse. He'd stood in the parking lot, staring after her car like a lovesick teenager until it was out of sight. Then it had been all he could do not to jump in his own car, chase her to her house, escort her inside and take up that hug at the dangerous point where it had ended.

He parked in his assigned space beside the building; then, deep in thought, made his way to his condo. After shutting his front door behind him, he found himself pacing back and forth in the living room. All along, he'd assumed that a different kind of relationship with Lindsay was impossible. What if that assumption was wrong?

He trotted out the biggest problem first: the possibility that if they became romantically involved, it might ruin their working relationship. That *was* a biggie, no doubt about it. But it was a far-from-inevitable consequence. They were good enough friends that they would survive the awkwardness if she should reject him out of hand. If she didn't reject him, then it was a matter of taking things gradually, while keeping the lines of communication open so that no misunderstandings or "lovers' quarrels" would be allowed to spill over into their work lives.

Lovers. The very word, applied to him and Lindsay, made a warm tide of sensual awareness flood through him, followed swiftly by a familiar tightening in his groin.

The only other thing, apart from the professional complications, was their age difference; and that, he dismissed. If she were twenty years older than he, instead of ten, then it might be a problem. Ten years was nothing.

That settled that. Sure, there was a risk. Wasn't there a risk in anything worth having?

He let out a groan. He must have been crazy about Lindsay for months, without even knowing it. So that's why the Bambis no longer attracted him.

Only one obstacle remained, and that *was* a biggie: convincing her that they were meant to be lovers.

With his accountant's tendency to want everything neatly laid out, he was sorely tempted to sit down and work out a detailed plan. That seemed too cold, too calculating—when all his thoughts about Lindsay were permeated with warmth. Instead, he decided, he'd wait and see—and be prepared to improvise.

BY THE TIME SHE got home, Lindsay had regained her mental equilibrium—pretty well. Except that she couldn't quite figure out what to do with herself.

She stood purposelessly in the living room of her house, looking at it as if she'd never seen it before. A long, pale peach couch with flower-printed cushions heaped on it was the focal point of the room. Flowery drapes in a matching print and an arrangement of silk tulips on the coffee table completed the motif.

After her divorce, Lindsay had redecorated the whole house, wanting to stamp it with her own personality. Now, suddenly, the living room looked too feminine. One quick glance, and an astute observer could easily deduce that no man lived here.

She left the living room and crossed through the kitchen. Entering the family room, she felt a little better. Here, everything was durable and plain, designed to withstand the activities of exuberant teenagers. She could probably redecorate this room now, too, considering that Dina would be home less and less as the years went by. And then the day would come when Dina wouldn't come home at all any more, except for occasional visits; she would have her own home, perhaps a husband, children.

Lindsay wrapped her arms around herself as a wave of loneliness swept over her. She didn't try to fight it off; she had learned that the best way to cope with these rare moments of self-pity was to give in to them, and cry if she needed to.

Before a single tear came, the phone rang. She picked up the family-room extension and sat down on the worn beige couch. "Lindsay, it's Adam Holloway."

"Hello, Adam. How are you?"

"Fine." He paused. "Well, actually, not so fine. It turns out I've got a problem with tomorrow night."

"Oh? I'm sorry to hear that," she said. Indeed, she should be sorry, but she couldn't say she felt any stabs of genuine disappointment. In fact, it was better this way; she'd have more time to spend with Dina—assuming Dina had no plans of her own for Saturday night.

"The thing is," Adam went on, "my ex-wife's mother is ill and my ex-wife needs me to take the kids this weekend."

Lucky woman! Her own ex-husband, Martin, had effectively vanished from her and Dina's lives. It wasn't entirely his fault, since his company had transferred him to New York. But she wished Martin could have made more of an effort to maintain a relationship with his daughter.

"I hope you understand," Adam said.

"Of course I do. Completely."

"Good. Thanks. What about next weekend instead? Are you free on Saturday night?"

One of the nice things about being almost forty, Lindsay thought, was that she didn't have to play games anymore and pretend to have to consult a crowded social calendar. "Saturday's fine."

"Great." Adam sounded genuinely delighted.

After a few more words of conversation, Lindsay hung up the phone. It rang again, almost at once. Hearing Joanne's voice, Lindsay kicked off her shoes and, with one hand, reached up to release the pins that held her hair in a chignon. Conversations with Joanne were rarely brief.

"I'm desperate," Joanne declaimed dramatically. "It's only a week until the benefit and I simply have to get more practice. I need a guinea pig, Lindsay."

"Okay, I'll volunteer. Why don't you come on over?" It was a good idea, now that she thought about it. If the demons of loneliness were still lurking, Joanne's presence would effectively banish them.

"I can't tonight," Joanne answered ruefully. "It's the last meeting of the planning committee for the benefit. How about tomorrow night?" Before Lindsay could reply, Joanne said, "Oh, no, I forgot. You have a date, don't you?"

"I *had* a date." She explained about Adam's call. "Dina'll be here tomorrow night, though."

"The more the merrier! I can practice on her, too."

Lindsay hesitated only a moment, deciding there was no reason Joanne shouldn't come. Dina liked Joanne and there'd be plenty of other times during the weekend for mother-daughter chats.

"I'll bring pizza," Joanne cajoled. "Pepperoni and extra mushrooms?"

"Sounds great," Lindsay said warmly. "About six?"

"Perfect. Say, I tried to call you earlier. Were you working late?"

"Not exactly. Tim and I had dinner after work."

"Tim didn't have a date? On a Friday night? That boy must be slipping."

"He says he's given up on the Bambis and I guess he really has. Apparently he isn't seeing anyone right now."

"Hmm," Joanne responded meaningfully. "Do you remember my friend from yoga class—April Maddox? Well, she's got this adorable daughter. She's twenty-three or -four. She'd be just right for Tim. Do you suppose there's any way you and I could fix them up?"

"I doubt it," Lindsay said. It *was* a good idea. In fact, she had actually met both April Maddox and her daughter. The girl *was* adorable—a blonde, which made her Tim's type—and she'd seemed bright. Fortunately there was an insurmountable obstacle to Joanne's plan, and Lindsay voiced it. "I'm fairly certain Tim wouldn't take kindly to being fixed up with anyone. He likes to choose his women friends himself."

"Oh." Joanne sounded disappointed.

Fortunately? Why had she thought it fortunate that Tim was un-fix-uppable? It was as if she wanted him for herself. Well, she did. At least, her body was foolish enough to feel what she'd felt during that moment when he'd hugged her. Even now, burned into her body's memory was the curve of his hand on her shoulder, the jut of his hip against her side, the sensation of his muscled thigh brushing hers. . . .

She repressed the memory. She couldn't have Tim. Nor had he shown any signs of wanting her.

Why *should* he? she chided herself. Men generally went for women younger than themselves, not ten years *older*. Even if he was the exception to the rule, there was their partnership, their friendship—both of which could be ruined by a romance gone wrong.

It occurred to her fleetingly that she'd been getting quite a lot of practice lately at stuffing Tim back into his appointed niche in her life. Her body and her emotions kept popping him out of place. Well, she'd work at regarding him only as a friend and partner.

Joanne was still talking, about the Mr. Right she had foreseen for Lindsay in her cards. "What do you think?

Could he be the guy you were supposed to go out with tomorrow night?"

"I have no idea. I hardly know the man."

"Don't forget, I'm counting on that lunch."

"I'll let you know," Lindsay promised.

After Joanne hung up, Lindsay felt restless. An awful lot of evening stretched ahead of her, needing to be filled.

Then she smiled. She knew exactly what to do with the hours before bedtime.

Talk about a busman's holiday!

Like a plumber who fails to fix his own stopped-up sink, Lindsay had a terrible time some years getting around to preparing her own tax return. For once she was going to get her records together well ahead of the deadline. Feeling busy and purposeful, she picked up her shoes and left the family room.

THE NEXT MORNING as Lindsay sat at the kitchen table sipping coffee and reading the newspaper, the phone rang.

"Tim!" she said, her astonishment reflected in her voice. He rarely called her at home, nor she him. There was no reason to, when they saw each other five days a week.

"It's me, all right." He seemed to be speaking rather loudly. In the background was a dull roar.

"What's going on over there, Tim?"

"What? I'm afraid you'll have to speak up."

She repeated her question in a louder voice.

"They've started construction across the way," he semishouted. "It's hell, I'll tell you. Trucks, cement mixers—you name it—they're all doing their thing right outside my window."

"They've started construction on Saturday?"

"What?"

"On *Saturday?*"

"I guess they're in a hurry on this one. Or trying to get the foundations laid while the weather's clear. Or something."

"Poor you."

"What?"

"I said, 'Poor you!'"

"Yeah, poor me. My quiet weekend's shot, that's for sure, though I assume they won't go so far as to work on Sunday, too. Listen, Lindsay. I was about to leave my place—and I remembered. Isn't Joanne's benefit today?"

What an awful liar he was. He knew full well that the benefit wasn't for another week. It had occurred to him that if Lindsay heard the background noise, she might take pity on him and invite him over to spend the day at her house.

"No, Tim. The benefit's not until *next* Saturday."

"Oh. Right. Too bad. I wouldn't have minded having something to do away from my place this afternoon." Talk about laying it on with a trowel!

She'd figured out how to pitch her voice so he could hear her. "What are you going to do?"

"Oh, I don't know," he said shamelessly. "I could always go to the office for a while. I'm sure I could find something that needs to be done."

"What a way to spend a Saturday!" She was silent for a moment. He thought he had her hooked, that she was going to invite him over. He could envision a lazy day. A long leisurely lunch somewhere. Maybe they'd take a walk. The weather was sunny but cool, and after the walk, they could curl up in front of a fire. . . .

Lindsay considered. Why not take pity on him? What harm would there be in Tim coming over, spending the day? She could fix sandwiches or something easy for lunch. Maybe in the afternoon, they'd drive out of the city, hike a bit somewhere where there was dirt instead of concrete underfoot.

She was on the verge of issuing the invitation when she heard the front door open and close. How could she have forgotten about Dina?

Her daughter's voice called, "Hey, Mom! I'm home! Where are you?"

She covered the mouthpiece of the phone. "In the kitchen, hon." Then she said to Tim, "I'm sorry. I'd better go. Dina just arrived."

As he hung up the phone, Tim slapped his forehead. How dumb of him! It had slipped his mind that Dina was coming home for the weekend. Naturally, Lindsay would want to spend time with her daughter without someone else around.

He smiled to himself as he walked to the door of his condo, almost as much pleased as he was disappointed. She'd *nearly* invited him over; he was sure of it. It seemed like a good sign—not that she'd willingly jump into his bed the minute he snapped his fingers. At least she didn't seem to balk at the thought of spending time with him outside office hours. It would take time. Lots of time.

He was still stuck with finding somewhere to go for the rest of the day. He might actually go to the office for a while. Afterward, he might take off for the Angeles National Forest. There were tall trees up there and paths to hike on. Best of all, blessed, blessed quiet!

JOANNE HELD OUT the tarot deck to Dina while Lindsay looked on. "Okay, hold the cards in your hand and think of the question you want answered," Joanne instructed. "You can tell me what the question is or not."

Dina's face took on a look of intense concentration and Lindsay gazed at her with maternal love and pride. Dina was turning out to be really pretty. She had Lindsay's dark hair—in Dina's case, worn short and permed. Her features were more like Martin's—a refined version. She had Martin's dark eyes—much more striking than her own nondescript greenish-gray ones. However, Dina seemed unaware of her attractiveness, and rather than exploiting her appearance with lots of makeup and revealing clothes, preferred to rely upon her mind and personality. She was really coming into her own.

She and Dina had spent the day together. A nice day, which had included lunch out, followed by browsing in the nearest mall. Something was bothering Dina. Several times, she had seemed about to mention it, but had pulled back and said something else.

Now the three women were grouped around the coffee table in the family room. Joanne had laid out the tarot cards and begun explaining the meanings of the individual cards to Dina without once consulting the book. She certainly was getting much better at it.

Dina didn't look too excited when Joanne started talking about the "guiding forces" behind all one's decisions.

They took turns with the cards several more times. By the end, Joanne was getting pretty slick, putting together a coherent reading with hardly any hesitation.

"You're going to be great at the benefit," Lindsay told her with enthusiasm.

"Thanks to you guys." Joanne glanced at her watch. "Whoops! It's getting late. I guess I'd better go."

There were hugs amid the goodbyes. Lindsay and Dina returned to the family room and curled up at opposite ends of the couch.

"She's such a kick," Dina said with a smile. "But I'm glad you're not like that. I don't think the tarot cards and astrology really can answer the important questions. Don't you agree, Mom?"

"I guess for some people it's a way to help think about things. Still, the big stuff, we all have to figure out for ourselves."

Dina nodded. "Those readings Joanne did for me didn't really help much."

At last, it looked like Dina was going to talk about what was bothering her. "You had a big question, I take it?"

Dina gazed down at her hands. "Well, not really big. I mean, it's not life-or-death." She paused. "I've been trying to figure out how you know if a guy's right for you."

"Hmm. That *is* a big question. Somebody you've been seeing?"

"I've been out with him a couple of times. He asked me out for this weekend, too." She glanced quickly at Lindsay, then away again. "I hope this doesn't sound bad, Mom. That's one of the reasons I came home. I didn't want to have to tell him yes or no." —

Lindsay said carefully, "It doesn't sound as if you're all that sure you like him."

"I'm not. I mean, I don't think I really *like* him very much at all. He's this jock, you know—really big on the track team—and all the girls in my dorm think it's so cool that he's asking me out." Dina wrinkled her nose.

"All he ever talks about is himself. When he's *not* talking about himself, it's stuff that's boring to me. Most of the time, I tune out when he's talking."

Lindsay swiveled on the couch so she was facing Dina. "Then what's the problem, hon? He sounds like he's a real jerk, and I'm sure you wouldn't keep dating him just because the other girls think it's . . . cool."

"Oh, Mo-om." The name was spoken with the old, reproachful, teenage inflection. "I have better values than that," Dina finished indignantly.

"I know you do, hon. That's what I said." Dina seemed mollified and Lindsay continued, "If that's the case, I feel like I'm missing something here. Why would you even consider going out with him?"

Dina flushed and bit her lip. "It feels really funny to say this to you, Mom. I mean, I know you'll understand and all, but still . . ."

Lindsay smiled. "Fire away, honey. I can take it."

"He turns me on," Dina said bluntly. "I mean, he's got this really great body and when he kisses me . . ." She rolled her eyes.

Uh-oh! Lindsay thought. Here was a genuine problem—one that she'd better find an answer for quickly. She was a fine one to be addressing that particular problem, considering how "turned on" she was by a man as wrong for her as the track jock was for Dina. Of course, there was a major difference; she *liked* Tim, liked him a lot. The basic principle was the same, however.

She dredged up all the motherly wisdom she could and began, "That physical response you're talking about is perfectly normal, as you know. We all get 'turned on' by certain men. But friendship—liking the kind of person a man is—is just as important as the physical part."

"Yeah, I know," Dina replied. "That's what's so weird. There's this guy in my world-history class. I like *him* a lot. I mean, when we get together, we have the most amazing conversations. He just doesn't . . ." She paused, obviously searching for a phrase.

"Just doesn't do it for you?" Lindsay suggested.

Dina nodded.

"Well, then, he's probably not the right guy, either. That spark's important, too, hon. What you have to find is *both*—a guy you really like, who turns you on."

"That's really *hard!*"

"I know," Lindsay said ruefully. "It *isn't* easy finding the right man. Don't ever let anybody tell you it is, or that it's okay to make do with somebody who *isn't* right. Not everybody would agree with me, but I think it's better to be alone than that."

Dina curled her legs up under her. "Is that why you haven't found anybody since you and Dad split up?"

"Mm-hmm."

Dina sighed. "Well, if you can hold out, I guess I can, too."

Lindsay smiled warmly at her. "It won't be as hard for you, honey. I promise. You're young, so there are more single men available to you, and you'll be meeting lots of guys at college."

"I know." She leaned forward and touched Lindsay's arm. "Thanks, Mom. I guess I knew all along what I should do about Rick—that's this jock guy—but it'll be easier now that we've talked about it."

Lindsay glowed. It wasn't often that a child Dina's age admitted that a parent had actually provided help. She savored the warmth of the moment.

Then Dina glanced at her watch. "Eleven o'clock. Want me to turn on the news?"

"If you like." Lindsay usually watched the late news; she'd done it for years. But if Dina would rather go on talking, she could certainly miss it tonight.

"Yeah, I think I do," Dina said. "It's sort of like...almost a ritual, you know. Makes me feel really at home." She jumped up and turned on the TV, then returned to curl up companionably beside Lindsay on the couch.

No major conflicts or overwhelming disasters had occurred since that morning, and terrorists of all stripes seemed to have taken the day off. She and Dina talked occasionally, commenting on what was being shown on the screen.

"Now for local news," said a newscaster who appeared to have been hired for his good looks rather than his reportorial skills. "In the San Fernando Valley community of Chatsworth, a parked truck loaded with building supplies lost air pressure in its brakes this evening and cut loose, rolling down a hill and crashing into a twelve-unit condominium."

Dina rose from the couch, half blocking Lindsay's view of the screen. "I think I'll fix some cocoa. You want some, Mom?"

Lindsay leaned sharply to the right to see around Dina. She gazed in horror at the tube. "My God!" she exclaimed. "That's Tim's place!"

4

DINA TURNED toward the TV. "Is it really, Mom? How can you tell? All those condo buildings look alike to me."

"Shh!" Lindsay said fiercely. Dina's voice had blotted out the newscaster's, except for a couple of words—"damages" and "injuries." Lindsay felt as if the runaway truck had slammed into her, too. Could Tim be hurt? If so, how badly? Cold chills ran up and down her spine. The thought of Tim broken, battered, was unbearable. Thank heaven the newscaster hadn't said that anyone had been killed.

The picture changed—from the two-story building, with the back end of a huge truck protruding from the side of a shattered wall, to an upper-body shot of Mr. Slick, with his blow-dried coiffure. "And on a lighter note..."

Dina gazed worriedly at Lindsay. "Why don't you call Tim, Mom? You can't be sure it really was his condo."

"I'm sure," Lindsay replied grimly. She had been to Tim's place—perhaps half a dozen times, to pick him up or drop him off when his car was in the shop, and to take him a casserole and a "Get Well" card from the staff, that time he had the flu. The general color, shape and size of the building, plus an interesting circular flower bed out front, made it unmistakable.

It had looked to her as if the truck had devastated the north end of the building, where Tim's condo was.

She grabbed the phone from the end table and dialed. It seemed to take forever before a recorded voice announced, "That number is out of service at this time."

Lindsay pressed down the button to disconnect. She had to call someone—someone who would know if Tim was all right. What were the names of his friends? Her mind was so fogged with fear, she couldn't think. While she was still holding down the button, the phone rang. She said a shaky hello into the receiver and at once heard Tim's voice. "Hi, Lindsay. It's me."

Weak with relief, she sagged back against the yielding cushions of the couch. "Tim!"

"I'm sorry if I'm calling too late. I just saw the story on the news and—"

"Thank heaven you called!" she interrupted. "I was so worried about you."

"Sorry. I would have called and told you about it earlier, but it didn't occur to me it'd be on the news until I saw it just now. I know you usually watch the eleven o'clock news and I thought I'd better call and let you know I'm okay."

Lindsay blinked. How had he known that about her? She couldn't recall ever having mentioned her nightly ritual. She must have said something about it at some point, and he had remembered. "Are you okay? Were you home when it happened? Wasn't it your place the truck hit, after all? It looked on TV as if it was."

"I'm fine. Everybody's fine. The guy who lives next door ended up with a few cuts and bruises, but that's all. I wasn't home—thank heaven!—because it *was* my place the truck hit. Darn thing had good aim. It made a perfect bull's-eye on my front door."

"But what will you do? Where are you now?"

"Don't worry. I won't be sleeping under a newspaper in the park. I'm in a motel right now and I guess I'll stay here until my place is rebuilt. The insurance company will pay for it." He paused. "At least, I think they will."

Dina was shifting from foot to foot, clearly impatient to hear what Tim had said.

"Just a minute, Tim." Lindsay covered the mouthpiece with her hand, and looked up at her daughter. "He's all right," she said, then relayed what Tim had told her.

Dina frowned. "He's staying in a motel? That's a drag. Or it will be, if it takes a long time to get his place fixed up." In a clear, ringing voice—a voice that might carry, even through Lindsay's muffling hand—she went on, "You ought to invite him to stay here, Mom, so he doesn't have to stay in an awful motel."

Lindsay stiffened. The reasonable part of her said: *Why not?* For that matter, how could she *not* invite Tim to stay? They were friends, and friends offered to help each other, especially when one friend had a big house with plenty of extra space and the other friend had just been made homeless.

Her other response was pure, unadulterated *fear*— the kind that sent adrenaline whizzing through the veins.

She didn't even have to ask herself what she was afraid of. She knew. It was that not-subterranean-*enough* attraction of hers to Tim that scared her. Having dinner with him had been too much fun and the wrong kind of fun. What would it be like, having him here in the house, sleeping across the hall night after night? Under those circumstances, how was she supposed to remember and *keep* remembering that Tim,

by virtue of his age and the fact that they were partners, was strictly off-limits, even as an object of fantasy?

Dina was watching her with a quizzical expression,
wondering why she was hesitating.

Tim was on the other end of the phone. If he'd heard
Dina's suggestion, he might be thinking...what?
Lindsay had no idea, because she couldn't guess
whether he'd *want* to stay here. He might hate the idea.

If he didn't hate it, she'd have to view his staying here
as an excellent opportunity for growth, because she'd
have to develop better control of her mind's wayward
thoughts and her body's wayward physical responses.
In any case, since he might have heard Dina's suggestion, she *had* to invite him.

She uncovered the mouthpiece of the phone and tried
to make her voice sound bright and enthusiastic. "Dina
had a great idea, Tim. Why don't you stay here while
your place is being rebuilt?"

There was only a momentary silence. The next sound
she thought she heard was a strange one, as if Tim had
swallowed. His voice was perfectly normal when he
replied, however. "It's really nice of you to offer, Lindsay. I'd like that a lot. I wasn't looking forward to
spending weeks in a motel. You're sure it's okay,
though? I wouldn't want you to feel you *had* to invite
me."

"I don't want you to feel you have to accept," she said.
"The offer is sincerely meant."

"In that case, gratefully accepted."

Accepted... If her earlier feelings had been mixed,
now she felt an absolute goulash of reactions. Delight,
fear, regret, anticipation—all jumbled together.

"When would be a good time for me to show up?"

She got a grip on herself. "Well, you're already set-tled in the motel tonight. How about tomorrow after-noon?" That would give her a chance to make sure the guestroom was in order. Because it was rarely used, the weekly cleaning lady went over it only occasionally.

"Any time in particular?" Tim asked.

Lindsay thought for a moment. She had promised Dina lunch out. "Anytime after two. How does that sound?"

"Fine. I'll see you then."

"See you," Lindsay echoed.

Tim hung up the phone, thinking that if he had known how to dance a hornpipe or a jig, he would have done so, heedless of the people sleeping in the motel room directly beneath his. Instead, he waved his fists in the air and proclaimed triumphantly to the empty room, "All *right!*"

He was glad, now, that he'd resisted the temptation to lay plots and plans to convince Lindsay that he and she should be lovers. He never would have factored into his calculations the possibility that fate, in the form of a large truck, would decide to intervene so benefi-cently on his behalf.

"I'M TAKING OFF, Mom." Dina's voice floated from downstairs up to the guest room where Lindsay was fussing over details she'd already checked a half-dozen times. Tim's room was as ready for him as it was going to be, and staring at it wouldn't make it any more or less so.

The double bed was covered with a quilted spread in the colors of autumn leaves. There was a big desk un-der the window, with a good reading light on it. The dresser had been completely cleared. The closet, except for hangers, was empty.

She went out onto the upstairs landing. Dina stood at the foot of the stairs, her backpack leaning against the wall next to the front door. "How come you're leaving so early?" Lindsay called down the stairs.

Dina gave her an odd look. "I told you yesterday. I've got some work I have to do at the library."

"Oh, right." She'd forgotten. Or had managed to forget. Wishful thinking had suggested that Dina would be around to help ease the awkwardness of Tim's arrival.

The word she'd mentally used took her aback. *Awkward?* Why should a friend coming to stay for a little while be awkward? She'd had houseguests in the past and had never had this jumpy feeling in her stomach, as if the President of the United States, and the entire royal family of England were all due to show up on her doorstep.

She hurried down the stairs and gave Dina a big hug. "Thanks for coming, hon. Let me know what happens with the jock." As she spoke, she thought she heard a car slowing on the street out front, then come to a stop. *Tim?*

Dina made a face. "I know what's going to happen. I'm going to tell him no the next time he asks me out."

"Good for you," Lindsay said, her ears finely tuned to the sound of a car door closing. Could she hear footsteps coming up the walk?

Dina rummaged through her backpack for her car keys, then drew them out, jingling, as the doorbell rang. She opened the door. "Oh, hi, Tim."

"Hi, Dina. Good to see you." His arms were full, a grocery bag in each.

".   od to see you, too. It's too bad about your place,
but I'm glad you're going to stay here." Dina chuckled.
"You can take care of my decrepit old mother for a
while . . . change the light bulbs and fix the faucets and
stuff. She's terrible about that sort of thing."

"Is she?" Tim asked, casting an amused glance at
Lindsay. "That's funny. As far as I know, your mom's
good at anything she does."

"Not faucets," Dina said blithely. "Well, gotta go.
Bye, Tim. Bye, Mom."

She brushed past Tim, who was still standing on the
doorstep, and hurried off toward her car.

"Nice kid," Tim remarked with a grin.

"I've always thought so," Lindsay agreed. "Too bad
she isn't going to live to reach twenty. 'Decrepit old
mother,' indeed!"

"You don't look a bit decrepit to me," he said with a
frankly admiring glance.

She didn't *feel* decrepit, either. And why should she?
Lindsay thought, when not only was she still dressed
in the nice gray slacks and lighter-gray silk shirt she had
worn for lunch with Dina, but had sneaked into her
bathroom ten minutes ago to renew her makeup and
check her hair.

The way Tim looked started an insistent flutter beneath her breastbone. It was rare for her to see him out
of his office clothes, and *out* was the operative word,
for Tim wasn't wearing much at all. January was being
its perverse self, providing torrential downpours for a
week, followed by days of hot, brilliant sunshine. This
was one of the latter and Tim had taken advantage of
it. A tank top revealed muscular upper arms—not
bulging in an unattractive, muscle-man fashion, but
rounded and firm. The sleeveless top's scoop neck an-

swered a question Lindsay had often wondered about—
whether Tim was smooth- or hairy-chested. He was just
right. Not overly furred, but not baby smooth, either,
with soft, chestnut-colored wisps below his collarbone.

If his upper half was pleasant to the eye, his lower half
was more so. He was dressed in running shorts that revealed long legs that were nicely fashioned, straight,
with good strong definition of the muscles in his calves
and thighs. For an instant, Lindsay's errant mind tossed
up an image complete with a rush of tactile sensations,
of one of those long, strong legs inserted seductively
between hers.

Oh, Lordy! she thought when she felt her own thigh
muscles clench in an involuntary response. Could she
make it a house rule that he was to remain fully clothed,
covered from shoulders to ankles, at all times?

One thing Lindsay had was poise. She could put it
on as if it were a new dress, displaying it no matter how
unsettled she felt inside. So her voice revealed not one
whit of her inner turmoil as she said "Come in, Tim,"
and stepped back to give him room to enter.

She glanced at the grocery bags he was holding. "It
was nice of you to think of it, but you didn't have to
bring your own supplies." No, indeed! She had shopped
maniacally that morning, before Dina was even out of
bed, piling everything into the shopping cart that she
could imagine Tim would want to have around the
house. They were now in shape to withstand even the
most prolonged siege.

Tim stepped into the cool foyer without replying. A
remark about still being a growing boy and not wanting to eat her out of house and home had formed on his
tongue, but he caught himself in time. It was a silly lit-

tle thing, but he didn't want to emphasize their age difference by referring to himself, even in jest, as a boy.

"Only one of them is groceries, actually." He nodded down at the bag he carried in his crooked right arm. "The other holds all my worldly possessions." This morning he'd gone shopping, which had helped to kill what had seemed like an endless stretch of time until the appointed hour for showing up at Lindsay's place. He'd acquired toilet articles, clean underwear, and a shirt and slacks he could wear to the office tomorrow if he had to. "They've got my condo cordoned off until some inspector gets around to deciding if it's safe to go inside," he explained. "I'm supposed to be able to check late this afternoon and see if I can get in to rescue some of my stuff."

"It must be awful," Lindsay said, "having your home destroyed like that."

"It's not my idea of a good time," Tim agreed. But definitely well worth it, if his being here gave him the means to demonstrate to Lindsay what their relationship could be—and should be. He'd have to go slowly, and work bit by bit to turn their friendship into something more. Going slow would be difficult. His awareness that the two of them were alone in the house made him want to hurry the process. He could put his two bags on the spindly little table next to the front door and dramatically sweep her into his arms and up the stairs to heaven.

Right! He'd only scare the wits out of her and make her rescind her invitation before he'd even unpacked.

Lindsay reached for the bag of groceries. "Why don't I stick that in the kitchen? I'll put them away after I show you to your room."

"Why don't we both take the groceries to the kitchen? Seeing my room can wait. You can show me where things go, and then I won't have to bother you every time I want to fix myself a sandwich."

"Good idea," Lindsay said.

"WOULD YOU LIKE a soft drink?" she asked him five minutes later, once the groceries had been crammed into her overpacked shelves.

"Sure. But I'll get it." Tim moved to the refrigerator and stopped with his hand on the handle. "I think we should talk about that, Lindsay."

"About soft drinks?" she asked wryly.

He laughed. "No. Not exactly." He opened the door to the fridge and leaned over to peer at the bottom shelf. "Good grief! Cola, cherry cola, ginger ale, orange, grape, root beer. I've never seen such a selection in my life."

"I wasn't sure what you liked."

"What a hostess!" He plucked off a cola from a six-pack. "You want something?"

"A cola. I'll get the glasses."

"No, I'll do it. You sit and relax."

When he'd served them both, he sat down across from her at the kitchen table. Resting his elbows on the table, he gazed seriously at her. "It's your hostessing I want to talk to you about, Lindsay. First off, I can't tell you how much I appreciate your inviting me to stay. I would have gone crazy being in a motel for weeks and weeks. That's the point. It *may be* weeks and weeks, if you can stand having me around—"

"Oh, I'm sure, I—" she interrupted.

He cut her off in turn. "You won't be able to stand me being here if you continue to treat me like a guest. 'Fish and guests begin to stink after three days,' you know."

"But it's—"

"Wait. Let me finish." He'd thought about the necessity for this speech on the way over here. It needed to be said, not just for the sake of making his stay easy for them both, but for the future. If she could learn to relax, accept his presence in her house, it might be easier for her to accept the new role he hoped to play in her life. "The only way this is going to work out is if you stop thinking of me as a guest who has to be waited on or entertained or catered to, in any way. I'm a pretty independent sort of guy. I can cook and I'll be glad to do my share. I can also clean up—after myself, and whatever else needs cleaning. I'm a whiz at laundry. I learned years ago about hots and colds and don't-mix-whites-with-colors and all that stuff."

This speech of his covered all the topics that might arise if a man and woman were just starting to live together. In so many ways, the situation was exactly that. With one major difference.

They were going to be living together, but *not living* together. Not sleeping together. Not physically involved. Roommates—that was how she'd have to think of it. Two roommates who just happened to be different genders.

He went on: "In short, I'll be most comfortable if you'll do whatever you'd do if I weren't here. Is that a deal?"

That made sense. Perfect sense. Now the only question was, could she do it? She'd better. If she was to spend every instant of the next however-many weeks feeling the same intense awareness of Tim's physical presence—and physical appeal—that she'd felt ever since Dina had opened the door to him, she'd turn into a blithering idiot.

"Okay, Tim," she said. "I'll make a deal with you. I won't treat you as a guest. I want you to feel free to come and go as you please, spend your time exactly the way you would if you were living alone." The truly magnanimous thing to say next was that if he wanted to bring a friend—a female friend—home, that, too, was quite all right. She couldn't bring herself to form the words. Awakening in the morning to find Tim and some Bambi having coffee in her kitchen was not something that bore thinking of. Or even worse, hearing the sounds of lovemaking from the guest bedroom. That would be intolerable, despite the fact that she had no right to feel that way.

"I mean, please don't feel you have to check in with me or tell me if you're going to be out late. I'm not your mother, after all."

He leaned forward and, without warning, covered her hand with his. The tingle Lindsay felt and the pervading heat spreading up her arm was wrong, all wrong. Still, she didn't pull her hand out from under his; the sensation was too pleasant.

Concentrating on that forbidden sensation, she barely noticed how serious Tim was when he said, "Believe me, Lindsay. I'm fully aware of that."

THE ANCHORMAN for the nightly news bared his perfect teeth and said good-night to his colleagues. Nine-and-a-half hours since Tim had become her roommate, and in Lindsay's opinion it was going quite well.

After their discussion of the ground rules for his stay, she'd asked him about the accident and he'd explained what had happened. Later that afternoon, he had called to find out whether he could get into his condo to conduct salvage operations. When informed he could, he returned with two full suitcases.

While he was gone, Lindsay had fixed a simple meal for them. After he had helped her clean up, they had spent some time discussing the coming work week. She had never thought she would like bringing business home, but it turned out to have its advantages. No need, now, for a hurried conference with Tim first thing tomorrow at the office. This might turn out to be a very handy arrangement, especially now that tax time was upon them.

But the evening hadn't been all work to make her a dull girl. Tim had discovered the Nintendo games she'd bought for Dina back when they were all the rage, and they had ended up competing avidly.

It hadn't been dull at all. In fact, she could hardly think when she had enjoyed herself more.

Her intense consciousness of Tim's physical presence hadn't receded an iota, however. Even though he was across the room in an easy chair, out of her direct line of sight, she was acutely aware each time he shifted position or moved his hand to turn a page of the back issue of *Practical Accounting* he was reading.

Thank heaven, he was more dressed than he'd been when he first arrived. Before making the trip to his condo, he had changed into crisp tan slacks and a yellow polo shirt. The only trouble was, it didn't seem to help much; once having seen those parts of Tim she had never seen unclothed before, she couldn't forget the physical appeal of the body beneath the clothing.

Now the part of the day she had been unconsciously dreading was upon her—bedtime. The trick was going to be to get to sleep without thinking of Tim and wondering what he wore to sleep in, or whether he was a sprawler or curled up in a ball. Did he read in bed, or did he snuggle right into his pillow and go off to sleep?

Then there were the other things people did in beds—the things she simply couldn't permit herself to think about in relationship to Tim.

She rose from the couch and was pleased that her voice sounded casual. "I think I'll pack it in."

He reached up and snapped off the floor lamp beside his chair. "Me, too. Tomorrow's going to come bright and early." He rose as Lindsay used the remote control to turn off the TV, and they left the family room together.

She'd never considered what it would feel like to climb the stairs with Tim beside her—climbing toward the most intimate portions of the house, whose main reasons for existing were sleeping and bathing and donning one's clothes . . . or removing them.

She tried to divert her attention from such thoughts by counting steps. Seventeen, eighteen, nineteen. She had never before realized what a long climb it was.

At the landing, she pasted on what she hoped would pass as a natural-looking smile. "Well, good night. See you in the morning."

Tim gave a little wave, and surely she was imagining something almost wistful in his voice as he said goodnight.

Ten minutes later, ready for bed, Lindsay remembered she hadn't put the chain on the front door. Tim was in the guest bath; she could hear the water gurgling in the sink. *Do what you would do if he weren't here.* In theory, when Tim had suggested it, it had seemed like a good idea—with a few flaws that had become increasingly apparent.

If he weren't here, she would hardly be listening, hardly be feeling his presence as if somehow the warmth of his body were penetrating the walls and affecting her own temperature.

If he weren't here, she'd probably just dash downstairs in her nightgown. Given the fact that he might emerge from the bathroom any minute, that was clearly out of the question. She grabbed a satiny, ivory-colored robe from the hook on her bathroom door, slipped it on and tied the sash. Now, if Tim *should* happen to be in the upstairs hall while she was going to or from downstairs, she would be perfectly decent.

SHE WAS perfectly breathtaking. Having heard Lindsay's soft-footed descent of the stairs, Tim reasoned that what goes down has to come up again, and he waited to leave the guest bath until he heard a faint creak on the staircase. In order not to miss hearing her ascent, he had opened the bathroom door a crack and so, when he stepped out onto the shadowy landing, it was in silence.

Her hair was down, falling in a dark cloud around her shoulders, and the ivory robe she wore—though its crossover front covered her completely—revealed the soft, full shape of her unfettered breasts. Seeing her like this, he felt an ache in his groin and another in the region of his heart.

Such a beautiful woman. How could he have been so blind for so long to how he really felt about her? Did he have any chance that eventually she might come to feel the same way about him?

She gave a little start when she saw him standing there. "Oh, Tim! I didn't see you."

"Sorry. I didn't mean to scare you."

"You didn't. Not really." Lindsay looked at him and her heart began pounding wildly. He had changed into a dark brown terry-cloth robe that ended several inches above his knees. Actually, even more of his legs had shown in the running shorts he'd worn that afternoon than was revealed now. But this was even worse— seeing him in his robe with perhaps nothing underneath. This was an intimate moment. Had things been different between them, it would have been the most natural thing in the world for them to retire to *one* bed instead of two.

Was she imagining the way he was looking at her— with desire? It was shadowy in the hall, and she might be mistaken.

She swallowed the lump of longing in her throat before saying "Sleep well, Tim," and then turned toward the door of her room.

Though his touch on her shoulder was brief, his hand seemed to burn into her and his voice was hoarse as he said, "Lindsay?"

She turned her head. "Yes, Tim?"

"I . . ." He hesitated. "Nothing. Good night."

TIM HAD NEVER in his life put such thought into the morning getting-ready-for-work ritual. From the moment his eyes opened, he had been aware that Lindsay was somewhere in the house, going through her normal morning routine.

He had lain awake for what felt like hours the night before. For a moment there in the upstairs hall, he'd come close to blowing it, to coming right out and telling her how he felt and how much he wanted her. Or *would* he have blown it? For an instant, he believed he saw desire in her eyes, too. If he was right, he'd missed an opportunity. He might have been wrong. All in all, it was better to wait a little longer, give her time to get used to his being here.

The timing could have been better for this campaign of his. From today right through the magical, glorious day—April 16th—he and Lindsay and their three accountants and two computer-entry people and Nancy would all be run off their feet. He and Lindsay would be working twelve- and sometimes fourteen-hour days.

Yet he couldn't quibble with fate by requesting that the truck slam into his condo at a more convenient date. Besides, he wouldn't have been able to wait until after mid-April, anyhow. Now that he understood how he felt about Lindsay, he had to act on it.

The moments after he stepped out of the shower and toweled himself dry were in some ways the most disorienting. At home, he would have pulled on his robe and gone to the kitchen to fix himself a cup of coffee. Here, he felt maybe he should get completely dressed first. Then he reminded himself of the deal he and Lindsay had made—that he should behave as if he were in his own home. The one concession he made was to pull on a pair of briefs under his robe.

IT WAS A GRAY and overcast morning—January doing another of its sudden reversals—and as Lindsay hit the switch to turn on the overhead light in the kitchen, she heard the pop and saw the flash that signal the death of a light bulb.

She gazed up at the source of the feeble glow insufficiently illuminating the room. Obviously, the most recently "departed" light bulb was following a trend started by its neighbor. Only one bulb out of three still shone.

If Tim saw that, he would know that Dina was right: Lindsay *wasn't* very good about faucets and light bulbs and sticky locks and a host of other little things. He might therefore feel it was his duty to turn into Mr. Helpful Handyman for the duration of his stay.

She sighed and went to the adjoining garage to get the stepladder.

THE SWINGING DOOR FLAPPED. "Good morning, Tim," Lindsay said without turning her head.

"Morning." Tim stared, entranced at the change in the kitchen's decor. The table had been shoved over nearer the sink and in the center of the room was a ladder with Lindsay up on the third step. Which put her slim, curving derriere in its narrow, navy blue skirt a little above his eye level and only a few feet away.

He took a step closer, wondering how *much* closer he could get without infringing on her personal space. "Need a hand?"

"No, I've got it." She was clearly well along in the procedure. He watched as she screwed the bolt back in that held the globe-shaped fixture to the ceiling. Then she began to descend, bringing mouth-drying feminine curves even nearer.

He couldn't help himself; he had to touch her. He decided he might manage it innocuously, under the guise of steadying her descent. "Careful," he warned, as if she'd tottered—which she hadn't—and put his hands on either side of her trim waist.

Did he feel her stiffen slightly in reaction? He couldn't be sure. At least she didn't flinch or pull away. He kept his hands on her until both her feet were on the linoleum—and a little longer than that.

It didn't mean a thing, Lindsay told herself fiercely. Tim was only being helpful, not seeking an excuse to touch her. She wished he hadn't done it. His hands were strong and very warm, especially above the waistband of her skirt, where the thin silk of her blouse was the only barrier between his skin and hers. His touch was firm; inherently masculine, somehow. She couldn't help thinking that were he to slide his hands only a few inches either up or down, the sensations would be even more erotic than the generalized heat she was feeling now.

He didn't actually let go. *She* stepped away from *him*, which made the sliding of his hands feel remarkably like a deliberate caress—a caress creating powerful sensations: a breathless swelling in her chest, a pulse of heat low in her body.

One part of her wanted to tell him not to do things like that so casually, so unthinkingly. That would be to admit how strongly his touch had affected her.

She cast a swift glance at him. He had no right to look so delectable, so early in the morning. He was wearing that accursed robe again and the effect of seeing him in it hadn't so far lessened through repetition.

His hair was slightly tousled, making it even more touchable-looking than usual. His eyes were bright. Obviously he'd slept well, which Lindsay hadn't. Not at all. It had taken all her willpower and considerable ingenuity to keep from slipping into a full-fledged fantasy of lying in Tim's arms instead of in her lonely bed. The only defensive measure that had worked had been to set her brain to figuring out tax strategies for clients in incredibly unlikely circumstances.

Despite extreme exertions of her willpower, her mind kept flashing images of Tim's arms around her, his legs entwined with hers, his mouth pressed hard and demandingly on hers. She had tossed and turned for hours.

She turned toward the ladder and began to fold it up. Tim jumped forward to help. "I'll take care of that," he said, and the awkward moment slipped away.

Breakfast was equally disturbing. It was the *lack* of awkwardness that got to her this time. Without fumbling or having to ask too many questions, Tim had made the toast the way she liked it, while Lindsay set out a couple of different kinds of cereal and poured the coffee she'd started earlier.

Not even the newspaper proved to be a problem— Tim seemed perfectly happy to bury his nose in the sports section while she scanned the front portion.

While Lindsay was flipping through the pages of the arts section for information about upcoming cultural events, Tim had cleared off the table and stuck the dirty dishes in the dishwasher. He was finished before she noticed, and that in itself was astonishing. When Martin *had* helped with things like that, it had been with clatters and flourishes to point out what an enlightened, extraordinarily supportive male he was.

Tim Reynolds might very well be the perfect man.

For someone else, of course. Not her. For someone younger—and not his business partner.

TEN MINUTES LATER—*crisis!*

They encountered each other on the upstairs landing. Lindsay thought of murmuring "We have to stop meeting like this," but decided against it.

Tim's hair was neatly combed or brushed or whatever he did to it that gave it such a look of springy vigor. Lindsay's fingers still itched to touch it, though it was no longer mussed.

Tim had his keys out, dangling from his hand. "We might as well take my car this morning, don't you think? Since it's out on the street."

Lindsay froze as the implications of his suggestion crystallized in her mind. "I don't know if it's such a good idea for us to ride to work together, Tim."

He looked genuinely puzzled. "Why not?"

There was an edge in her voice as she said, "Obviously, it hasn't occurred to you that people might get the wrong impression if they see us driving up in the same car. Not strangers—that wouldn't matter. But, what if some of our employees saw us?"

"What 'wrong impression'?" Tim asked innocently. "If anybody even notices or cares, they'll think I'm staying at your house because my place is a pile of rubble."

Lindsay looked down at the carpet and mumbled, "Well, I just think it would be easier if we didn't have to explain."

"We don't *have* to explain. Not a thing. We're adults and our living arrangements are nobody's business but our own."

That was true, though not really as simple as he made it sound.

"However—" his voice softened and he took a step closer "—there's really not much choice, Lindsay. We'll have to tell Nancy and the others that I'm staying with you, in case someone needs to get in touch with me outside working hours. Don't worry. I'll explain why."

"Oh . . . right," she said. "I didn't think of people needing to get in touch."

"THIS WAS REALLY NICE of you, boss," Nancy mumbled, her mouth full of bagel. She swallowed and waved a hand at the table in the supply room. "What a spread!"

Lindsay and Tim had gotten a little carried away at the bakery cum deli where they'd stopped on the way to work. In addition to the bagels and cream cheese they'd originally planned on, they'd bought lox to complement that particular treat, plus five different kinds of sweet rolls.

"It was really Tim's idea," Lindsay said.

Nancy gave Lindsay a conspiratorial wink. "Speaking of Tim . . . It's none of my business, boss, but didn't I see you getting out of his car this morning?" Her penciled-on eyebrows arched. "Something wrong with your car?"

Perfect, Lindsay thought sarcastically. Just the kind of question she'd been so looking forward to. Furthermore, Jack Bartlett, recently out of college and starting the two years of work experience he needed to qualify as a CPA, was standing only a few feet away, munching on a cinnamon bun. He *appeared* to be listening to Mary Chan, the office manager and bookkeeper. With Jack, you never knew. In his two months in the office, he had poked and pried into everything. Lindsay figured that if he didn't pass his CPA exam, the CIA would take him in a flash.

"Well, you see, Nancy," she began awkwardly, meaning to explain what had happened to Tim's condo.

Tim materialized at the absolutely perfect moment. He looped his arm around Nancy's waist. "Didn't Lindsay tell you? She deserves a Good Samaritan award." He explained about the accident. Most of the employees had seen the news, but hadn't connected it with Tim, so the questions and comments veered away from Tim's current living arrangement to what had happened to his condo.

No matter that she agreed—in principle—that she and Tim were both adults and that what they did was no one's business but their own; still, she wasn't prepared to deal with speculative glances and unspoken questions.

She was spared for only a few moments. A general reshuffling of people took place and Lindsay ended up in the hall outside the storage room, with Nancy again at her side.

The older woman winked. "So Tim's staying with you. Good for you, boss. I wondered when you'd do something about it."

Lindsay frowned. "About what?"

"About Tim," Nancy said, jerking her head in the direction of the storage-room doorway, where Tim was now talking to Jack Bartlett and Ernie MacIntyre, who handled the books for some of the small businesses who depended upon Ames and Reynolds, CPAs, for their accounting needs.

Nancy's second wink was even more suggestive than her first. "I wish I'd had the smarts you do, when I was your age. Forty's prime for women for, you know. That's exactly the time of life when you need a guy who's in *his* prime, too. Live it up, that's what I say."

Lindsay's mouth opened. What in the name of heaven was she supposed to say? Thank Nancy for the compliment on her supposed "smarts"? Or upbraid her for suggesting that Lindsay was using Tim as an unpaid gigolo? Or point out that she had her facts wrong; that if the magazines were to be believed, Tim, at twenty-nine, was a good ten years past his physical prime.

Not that she would ever have a chance to find out to what extent his prowess had deteriorated thus far, she assured herself.

She eyed their valued employee and said candidly, "Frankly, Nancy, I don't know whether to be flattered or furious. In any case, you've got it wrong. Tim and I are friends, nothing more. Got it?"

"Got it," Nancy replied, looking suitably chastened. "I'm really sorry, boss."

It was only later that it occurred to Lindsay to wonder if Nancy meant she was sorry for saying what she'd said—or sorry it wasn't true. At that moment, Tim's voice interrupted. "Attention, folks."

They'd both agreed it was his turn this year to make the opening-of-the-tax-season "Go get 'em" speech. She was glad he was doing it, particularly as she listened to him remind the staff of the principles Lindsay and Tim had agreed upon when their partnership was formed: Dedication to the client's best interests; an insistence on playing by the rules; unfailing courtesy. She doubted if she could have done half as well at injecting humor into the remarks, while still conveying the necessity for hard work and attention to detail during the coming weeks.

Then Tim concluded, in ringing tones, "Man—and woman—the battle stations, folks. The onslaught begins."

THIRTY MINUTES LATER, Nancy brought Lindsay a note. Written on the slip of paper in Tim's firm, unnmistakable hand, were two words: "Bird seed."

Mr. Goodall strikes again, Lindsay thought, and burst out laughing.

5

FOR ONCE, the madness of tax season was a blessing, Lindsay thought three days later, as she cleaned up her desk after her last appointment. With clients coming and going, there wasn't time to think—during office hours, anyway—about her current home life. Not that it wasn't pleasant. That was the problem; the evenings she and Tim had spent together had been far *too* pleasant—the laughter, the sharing of the day's experiences, the way their eyes seemed to meet so often in meaningful connection.

And there was the way he touched her—putting his hand on the small of her back for a moment as they cleared up after dinner, taking her arm as if she needed guidance or protection going through a doorway as they left a room together, reaching over to touch her hand to emphasize a point as they talked.

If she hadn't known better, she would have said he was *courting* her.

There was a knock on her office door and Tim came inside. "Ready to go?" he asked, with a big grin that made her heart flip-flop.

The smile she gave him was perilously close to the silly, besotted smile of a woman in love—she knew how it must look from the way it felt spreading across her face. She couldn't go on this way, or she would end up making an awful fool of herself.

Tonight, she decided, she would retire to her room early. Right after dinner, she would go upstairs, claiming she had some reading she wanted to catch up on. Perhaps if they spent less time together, she'd be better able to control the effect of his presence in her life.

LINDSAY AMES, *you're weak, weak, weak!* It was nearly ten, and Lindsay had just remembered the decision she'd made earlier—not to spend the whole evening with Tim.

They'd started talking.... Over dinner, Tim had told her about his family and his childhood. It would have been rude to interrupt, especially since what he was revealing fascinated her.

She'd done a fair amount of talking, too—mostly about *her* childhood. She'd been an only child and had never minded not having siblings. After hearing Tim's tales of growing up in a family of four brothers and two sisters, she now felt she had missed out, and she said so.

"There were times I would cheerfully have traded places with you," Tim replied.

They were sitting a couple of feet apart on the couch in the family room, each of them half turned toward the other. Tim had his arm resting along the back of the sofa, with his fingers dangling a few inches from her shoulder.

Though Lindsay was listening intently to what Tim was saying, a part of her was vividly aware of his hand, of how easy it would be for him to touch her.

He laughed. "Frankly, I still sometimes feel that way, when we all get together and everybody's talking and arguing. But most of the time, I figure I had a pretty good deal."

"I think I did, too," Lindsay said. "Basically, I liked being an only child."

"What about your parents?" Tim asked. "I assume they're still around."

"Oh, yes. They travel most of the time, since my father retired. Right about now, they should be in Cancún, soaking up the sun. They're having a great time."

Tim smiled. "They must be very proud of you."

"I think for the most part they are," Lindsay answered slowly. "Although my mother nearly had heart failure when I told her Martin and I were getting a divorce. She said she'd been raised to believe that marriages lasted a lifetime."

"And what did you say?"

"That I'd been raised to believe the same thing, as she very well knew, but that marriages didn't always work out."

He leaned a fraction closer to her and stared into her eyes. "What about your divorce, Lindsay? It must have been pretty rough."

She paused for a moment, wanting to give him an honest answer. "All in all, it was pretty smooth, pretty amicable."

His eyebrows arched upward. "Is that why you've never seemed to be as bitter as some people are?"

"I guess. Martin and I married when we were both sophomores in college. We decided we'd grow up together, but the problem was that we grew apart instead of together. We had less and less to say to each other, less and less connection with each other's lives—except for Dina, of course. And frankly, Martin's one of those men who might have been a great father to a boy, but he didn't know what to do with a girl." Funny, how easy it was to tell Tim all these intimate things.

"That's too bad." He hesitated, then asked, "Was there anything in particular that ended the marriage?"

Lindsay nodded, not at all reluctant to go on. "Six years ago, when Martin's company transferred him to New York, I realized that I didn't want to go. I decided that my relationship with Martin wasn't a good-enough reason to uproot my life. When I told him how I felt, he didn't exactly say so, but I think he was actually relieved. We parted friends." She frowned. "The only thing I resent is that he seems to think that when he and I divorced, he divorced Dina, too. He hasn't seen her in over a year now, and then it was only because he had to come out here on business. Plus he hardly ever calls her. I worry that her father's rejecting her like that may have warped Dina in some way."

"She doesn't seem warped to me. In fact, Dina seems like a pretty healthy kid."

"I hope so. I've done my best. I guess that's all anyone can say. Whatever happens to her now is—"

The words hit a sudden barrier in her throat as she felt a feather-soft touch skimming from her cheekbone, down the curve of her jaw to her chin—Tim's knuckles oh-so-gently brushing her face.

As she slowly turned her head to look at him, the back of his hand remained in contact with her skin. His face was very close and his hazel eyes had darkened, as he fixed his gaze intently on her.

His voice was soft and husky. "As far as I can tell, your best has been first-rate, Lindsay. Not just with Dina, but in everything you do." He fell silent for an instant. Lindsay knew she should use his momentary hesitation to pull away from him, but she was mesmerized, held not only by his touch, but by the compelling expression in his eyes.

"No, not just what you do," he went on. "What you are, the kind of person you are. The kind of woman." He inhaled deeply. "I've never really said this before, Lindsay, because the office hasn't seemed to be the right place for it and because I've never been able to find the right words to tell you how I feel, but . . ."

Lindsay drew in a long painful breath. "Tim, I . . ."

He had both hands cupped around her face now. "Wait. Let me finish." Again, he paused. "I still can't find the right words."

Dammit all! He couldn't say what he so desperately wanted to say. *I want you. I need you. I'm crazy about you. I think I'm falling in love with you.* Not yet!

It would shock Lindsay. As far as he could tell, she had never considered him in those terms, though there had been hopeful little signs during the past few days. Right now, it seemed best to let his body speak for him.

He left his hands on her face, threading his fingertips into the hair at her temples. Then he bent his head.

Lindsay was still mesmerized, her eyes wide open as Tim's face descended . . . closer, closer. Her eyelids drifted shut as his mouth touched hers. His lips were soft and smooth and at first the contact was delicate, a mere salute of lip to lip. Then his mouth began to move on hers—in tiny motions—slidings, nibblings—that were incredibly erotic.

The surge of warmth and excitement that spread throughout her body as he went on kissing her made her involuntarily lift her hands and grip his shoulders. One of her hands crept around the back of his neck. As she felt the stiff short hairs at the base of his head prickling her fingertips, she thought: *This is wrong! Crazy! This is Tim. Ten years younger. My business partner.*

All her thoughts scattered when the tip of his tongue penetrated her mouth. The result was dizzying. Myriad sensations swirled throughout her body. Her nipples tingled; desire, heavy and hot, pulsed in her lower body; and she couldn't prevent her own tongue from meeting his, sliding over and under, then darting out to flick between his teeth.

It was the sound in the back of his throat that stopped her, even though hearing that groan of need only heightened her own response.

She pulled away from Tim, conscious of her puckered nipples thrusting against her bra and of the heat and wetness between her thighs. She drew a deep breath, fighting for control, then said quietly, "We shouldn't have done that, Tim."

Tim hated hearing her say that, but he didn't hate the "we." Some women would have tried to pin all the responsibility on the male, but he should have known Lindsay wasn't like that. He looked down at her. The signs of passion were unmistakable—as if after the way she'd kissed him, he needed any evidence that she wanted him. Her pupils were wide and dark, her breathing unsteady; her cheeks and throat, flushed.

Her lovely throat was even more so, now that it was colored with desire for him. He lifted his hand and ran his fingertips from below her ear to the hollow of her collarbone.

"I don't agree," he said, not challengingly, just with certainty that he was right. "In my opinion, we should have done exactly that and more, a long time ago."

What was he saying? Lindsay wondered. Did he mean he'd thought of kissing her before he moved in here? If so, he'd never shown it—not in any way she'd been able to recognize.

She got to her feet, knowing that her only hope of thinking clearly was to put some distance between them. She crossed the room and at the far wall, next to the TV, stood for a moment with her back to him, gathering her resources. Then she turned.

She had to convince him that a physical relationship between them was wrong, because if he ignored her reasons and kissed her again, she'd be lost. Lost in desire, in liking and caring for this man, in the special feelings she'd had for him for so long now.

"Surely you see why that was a mistake," she began.

"Give me one reason." He sat back on the couch, one leg crossed over the other. Irrationally, Lindsay resented him for sounding and looking so calm when she was in turmoil.

"I can give you dozens. First of all, that—that kiss would never have happened except for the circumstances. You staying here, I mean. Propinquity, that's all it is. And it's not a very good reason for getting involved with someone."

"Wrong," Tim stated flatly.

"What?"

"I said, 'Wrong'! Propinquity may not be the greatest reason to kiss somebody—you may be right about that—but that's not what it is." Without warning he leaped to his feet, and now Lindsay could see that she'd misread him. He wasn't calm at all: not physically, for a bulge straining the front of his trousers showed that their kiss had had no less an effect on him than on her; and not mentally, either, for when he spoke, his voice was low and vibrant with intensity. "I wanted you before I came to stay here. I think I've wanted you for a long time, though I only let myself admit it recently. So it may just be propinquity for you, Lindsay, but it's not for me. It's much more than that."

He was standing only a short distance away and she could feel the heat rolling off his body, like a physical caress. She had to struggle to keep from stepping forward to fit herself against him, flatten her breasts against his chest and savor the prod of his obvious arousal against the soft flesh of her stomach.

She held herself back by exerting what felt like superhuman control. And she couldn't respond to his last statement that it might just be propinquity for her. She couldn't tell a lie and say she'd never been physically attracted to him before; nor could she tell the truth— that she'd desired him for an equally long time. To admit that would make her even more vulnerable than she already felt.

She brought her arms up and crossed them over her chest, knowing Tim would read the defensiveness of her body language, but needing some barrier between them.

"That's not all," she said. "There are other reasons."

"Go ahead."

"This is probably the most important one."

His eyebrows lifted, then fell. "I know exactly what you're going to say, Lindsay."

"Do you?"

"I think so." He shoved his hands in his pockets. "Our partnership. The dangers of mixing business and romance."

She nodded, glad to know that he could be reasonable about this. "That's it, exactly."

"I've thought a lot about that. And the conclusion that I've come to is that it doesn't have to be a problem."

She blinked in astonishment. "How could it *not* be a problem?"

He pulled his hands from his pockets and gestured as he spoke. "Because our friendship came first. In my opinion, it's a good, solid one. And I'm pretty sure you feel the same way."

She nodded. That much was undeniably true.

"Because I'm not talking about a one-night stand here. Or even a brief fling. I want a real relationship with you, Lindsay. Something big, something important. As far as I'm concerned, that's worth any risk we might be taking with the partnership." Before she could comment, he went on. "And most of all, I just don't see why there'd have to be any problems. The key, I think, is honesty. Complete honesty. Letting each other know how we're feeling, what we're thinking." He let out a strained laugh. "I'll tell you what *I'm* feeling right now. I want to kiss you again, a few dozen times, and then I want to take you upstairs to a big, cozy bed, where I want us to do wonderful things to each other. How's that for honesty?"

Lindsay felt her knees buckle. To desire and to *be* desired so forthrightly was a will-destroying combination. She forced herself to stiffen her bones and muscles. "Pretty honest," she admitted. "I don't know, Tim. Your reasoning sounds okay—right now. But I'm not sure it's really as sensible as I think it is at this moment."

"I understand. I've had more time to think about this than you. As I told you before, this isn't exactly a new idea to me."

He was right about one thing. If they were to have a relationship without it destroying their business, their partnership, they would have to be completely honest with each other. Might as well start that part of it now.

Feeling as if she were surrendering whatever armor she had left against him, she said, "Well, to tell you the truth, it's not exactly a new idea to me, either."

His eyes lit up. "Really?"

She nodded slowly. "I've been attracted to you for a long time, Tim. But I've told myself that it was wrong."

He closed the remaining distance between them and put his arms around her. She felt their strength and security, and a bubble of pleasure formed inside her as he said, "You don't know how happy I am to hear that, Lindsay—not that you thought it was wrong, but that you felt something for me."

"Oh, I did," she confessed. "I definitely did."

He unwrapped one arm from around her to tip her chin up. "Anything else you want to say before I kiss you again?"

"No, I . . ." She stared up into his eyes; then, with a little start of surprise, dropped her gaze and said quickly, before his lips touched hers and she was lost again, "Yes. Yes, there is one more thing I want to say. Maybe more than one."

He closed his eyes for an instant. "Okay, I guess I can hold off kissing you for a little longer."

She had to put it bluntly; there was no other way. "Have you considered that I'm too old for you, Tim?"

"Huh?" He drew back, obviously startled. "So I'm a few years younger than you. What's that got to do with anything?"

"It has . . ." She let her voice trail away. Maybe it didn't have anything to do with anything. She was healthy, fit, not exactly ready for the rocking chair and the knitting yet. The real problems that would arise would come down the road—if he wanted children, for instance. And later on, when he would be a vigorous man of fifty and she, at sixty, would be verging on elderly. Those were things she couldn't mention. Tim had said he wanted a relationship. That didn't mean he was talking about marriage, a long-term future; and to say anything that indicated she was thinking along those lines would be presumptuous indeed.

"I guess it doesn't matter. Not all that much," she said.

"You're darn tootin', lady." He bent toward her again.

She put up a hand, touching her fingertips to his lips. "But, Tim, I really need to think about some of these things—quietly, calmly—alone."

"I understand," he replied gravely. "All I want to do is kiss you one more time, and then we'll call it a night."

TEN MINUTES LATER, they stood kissing on the upstairs landing outside her bedroom door. There had been one more kiss and one more after that and then perhaps a dozen on the way up the stairs. Now he had his arms around her waist. Laughter sparkled in his eyes as he said, "One more, Lindsay."

"I'm going to hold you to that," she told him severely.

This one last kiss was like the others: intoxicating. His tongue probed her mouth and she found herself answering with probes of her own, reveling in his taste and texture. His arms tightened around her, pulling her lower body against his; his erection pressed, hard and demanding, into her belly. She could feel the shape and size of it even through all their layers of clothing. Her internal muscles opened, begging hungrily to feel him inside her, while her yearning hands grasped and kneaded the muscles of his back.

He let go of her without breaking the contact of their lower bodies, then moved his hands between them and lightly brushed her breasts. She arched her back, thrusting her sensitized nipples against his palms. She was drowning in desire. Dimly she recognized that if she was to think this thing through before she and Tim made love, she would have to break away from him now—or it would be too late.

Then he did exactly what she'd fantasized when she first got a good look at his lean, bare legs. He turned slightly, bringing one knee up between her thighs. The skirt she'd worn today was pleated so there was no hindrance to his pressing the top of his thigh against her pubic mound. The rush of sensation was so acute, she felt as if she was moving rapidly toward climax and release from the mere pressure alone.

Oh, Lord! If they did make love, would he find her too voracious, too hungry? For the first time, she regretted her long period of celibacy—though she had a hunch it made no difference at all. She could have been Rosie Roundheels for the past six years and she would still have desired Tim as acutely as she desired him now.

He rubbed his knee back and forth and Lindsay could feel the sensations building, building. Was it too late to stop? Would she not be granted time to think, to feel right about this, after all? Her fault, just as much as his. She was clinging to him, urging him on.

She was still clinging to him when he removed his leg from between her thighs and planted his feet squarely on the floor, putting a few inches of distance between them. She let go of him, realizing that his breathing was as ragged as her own. He gave a dazed shake of his head. "I'm sorry. That really wasn't fair. I know you wanted time to think." As if he feared what would happen if he stayed near her, he backed up. "Do you still want time, Lindsay? I don't want to be a . . . a tease, either, if that's the right word."

"Yes," she said huskily, though she wasn't certain she was telling the truth. "Yes, I do want time."

"Then, good night." He tipped her a salute, turned, and headed for the guest-room door.

Lindsay stood there, her mind fighting her body's urges, until his door had closed. Even then, it was all she could do not to go to him. A scratching on the door would be all it would take, she knew, to bring him to her.

How many regrets would she have had in the morning, if she'd had no chance to consider? Not whether it was foolish or wise to make love with Tim—she knew it was foolish and risky and dangerous to their partnership and to her heart. But whether it was folly of the suicidal order or merely survivable folly—that, she'd better decide before anything irrevocable happened.

TWO HOURS LATER, she was still awake. About an hour ago, it had struck her that if she had been convinced of the wrongness of going to bed with him, she should have asked Tim, right after that first kiss, to move out of her house. It might have been awkward for a while at the office, but they could have weathered it.

It had never even crossed her mind.

She was hooked on Tim. Addicted to being with him, to his companionship, to his presence around her house. Add that to the intensity of the physical response she felt in his arms, and what were all her rational objections worth?

She was good at sums; she knew the answer without thinking. She made a circle with her thumb and forefinger and held it up in front of her eyes.

Zero.

IT WAS THE MIDDLE of the next afternoon. "You should get your return within two weeks," Lindsay said to her elderly client as she ushered him to the door.

He smiled and gave a courtly if creaky bow. "Thank you very much, Ms. Ames. I must say, this is the first time in nearly sixty years of getting my taxes done that it's actually been a pleasure."

As soon as the door had closed behind him, Lindsay leaned back against it, muffling her laughter with both hands. Once she realized who he was, it had been all she could do to go through this new client's income and deductions without giving in to a fit of the giggles.

Still chortling, she hurried back to her desk, picked up the phone, and dialed a familiar number—Joanne's.

"Guess what," she said without preamble. "I've just met Mr. Right—the one your tarot cards promised. Remember?"

"Of course, I remember," Joanne replied, then added smugly. "I've been expecting this. The cards never lie." Her voice changed to a tone of breathless anticipation. "Now, tell me, who is he? Where did you meet him?"

"At the office. He just left. He's definitely tall, dark and handsome." All true. Her latest client had topped six feet by several inches. His hair was dark, though clearly owing its color to a bottle. And he was very attractive, for a man his age. "His name is Clement—"

"Clement? *Clem?*" Joanne interrupted. "It's not a great name, but I guess it's okay."

"You didn't let me finish," Lindsay told her. "His name is Clayton Wright. With a *W*. Mr. Wright. And he's eighty-two years old."

Joanne harrumphed. "Very funny."

"Absolutely true. I'll swear on a stack of Bibles."

"Hmm. So, what you're saying is that the cards told the truth."

"In a manner of speaking."

"Then, according to my calculations, you owe me lunch."

For Joanne's benefit, Lindsay let out an exaggerated sigh. "I guess you got me."

"I sure do, and I mean to collect as soon as possible. Let's see—the benefit's Saturday. You *are* coming, aren't you?"

"I wouldn't miss it," she said loyally.

"Then, how about I collect on your bet on Sunday?"

"Fine," Lindsay agreed. "Start thinking where you want to go. But remember, I'm only a poor, humble working girl. My budget can't take too much strain."

"Poor! humble! my foot! You guys are raking it in, this time of year. Say how's it going with Tim staying at your house?"

Lindsay felt a tingle at the mere mention of his name. Early in the week, she'd called Joanne to tell her what had happened to Tim's condo and that he'd be staying with her for a while. But that had been *before*. Before Tim had kissed her and made it plain what he wanted from her.

Though she'd dealt with today's clients well enough, all day, in the back of her mind, had been thoughts of Tim. Lindsay had gone over and over the arguments against having a physical relationship with him. They held. It *was* dangerous to mix business and romance.

And she was still ten years older than he, and always would be. But the bottom line was that she wanted him too much to deny the possibility of making love with him.

"Yoo-hoo! Lindsay?" Joanne's voice from the phone penetrated her thoughts. "What happened? Where'd you go?"

"Oh, sorry!" Lindsay responded, then lied shamelessly. "Nancy came in with something I had to look at. What were you saying?"

"I just asked you how it was going with Tim staying at your house."

"Fine," Lindsay said blandly. "Just fine."

A few minutes later, she hung up the phone, glad she had a break between clients. Okay. So she was very likely going to say yes to Tim. Tonight.

Which led to a new problem: protection. She hadn't had to do anything about that in a long time. And there was no simple answer. Her doctor had advised her against using either the Pill or an IUD. Those little sponge dealies they sold in drugstores—how well did they work? And then there was the safe sex issue....

She groaned. Having to think about these things was unpleasant, but not to think about them would be irresponsible—assuming she really was going to do what she'd been thinking about doing. With all those reasons not to, including the problem of protection, there hardly seemed to be any good reasons *for* making love with Tim, except that she wanted to.

At that exact moment, there was a soft tap on her door and the very cause of her speculations walked into her office.

All the air whooshed out of her lungs as she looked at him. She hadn't seen him since this morning when they'd driven in to work together—a drive accomplished in near-total silence.

Now she looked at him—his body tall and straight, the broad shoulders that did nice things for his brown sport coat; and his long, well-made hands, with blunt, clever fingertips that last night had seemed to know exactly how to touch her.

At that thought, a wave of heat moved through her. There was that desire! It was mild now, but she knew if he were to touch her again, it would become an irresistible force.

Her voice sounded strained as she said "Hi. How's it going?"

"Okay."

"Well, I just thought I'd say hello," Tim replied uncomfortably. "I guess I'd better get back to work."

Lindsay started to say "See you later," but bit back the words. Even *that* innocuous comment seemed too fraught with meaning to be uttered now.

IT WAS NO BETTER on the way home. Tim was silent; Lindsay was, too.

She hated this awkwardness with Tim, hated that just talking to him now seemed like a herculean task.

Even changing into more comfortable clothes once they reached her house became an issue. She didn't want to send the wrong message to Tim via her choice of clothing, and since she didn't know what message she *did* want to convey, how was she supposed to decide what to wear?

She finally selected the most neutral outfit she could find—the same gray slacks and shirt she'd worn the day Tim moved in. The final absurdity was that she also felt it necessary to check her hair, deciding to leave it the way she'd worn it at the office today, in a neat chignon.

She came downstairs to find Tim opening the door to a pizza deliveryman. He paid and took the box, then turned to Lindsay as he shut the door. "I hope you're in the mood for pizza. It seemed like . . . a good idea."

"Excellent idea," she said. At least they wouldn't be spending much time working together in the kitchen tonight. She wouldn't miss the easy banter that had become their dinner-fixing pattern over the past few days.

In the kitchen, she set out plates, knives, napkins and glassware in silence. Silently, Tim shredded lettuce for a salad. "Thousand Island?" he asked when he was done.

"Ranch for me tonight," was Lindsay's "eloquent" response.

Fifteen minutes later, they had exchanged four more lines of scintillating dialogue. Tim's had been: "Do you want one from the mushroom side or the pepperoni?" and "Ready for another slice?"; to which Lindsay had respectively replied, "Pepperoni, please," and "No, thanks."

It had been all she could do to cram one tasteless slice down and pick at the salad. She couldn't stand this much longer. Her mind was still whipping her back and forth between yes and no, as if she were strapped to a giant pendulum.

She got up, took her plate to the sink, then turned back to the table, her route taking her within a couple of feet of Tim.

Without warning, and without rising, he caught her by the wrist. "I *hate* this," he said forcefully. "I hate the way we are with each other today."

Lindsay inhaled sharply, then let out a long, slow breath before admitting, "I'm not too crazy about it myself."

"I thought I could deal with giving you some time to think, but I didn't think it would be like *this*."

"I didn't, either. Why is it, Tim? Why are we having so much trouble just talking to each other?"

He gave a little tug, and without quite knowing how it had happened, she found herself sitting in his lap. He wrapped his arms loosely around her. "That's better," he told her. "I don't know how it is for you, but *my* problem is that all the time, every single second, I'm wondering what you're thinking. 'Is she letting those so-called reasons why we shouldn't get involved get in the way of her feelings? What *are* her feelings? Does she care at all? How much does she care?'"

She had turned her head so she could see his face, and the wry grimace he made was both humorous and heartbreaking. "It just goes on and on," he said.

"Oh, Tim." She put one arm around his neck. "It's pretty much the same for me. All day, I've been thinking and thinking and thinking. It sounds as if we should give the clients we saw today a rebate. They sure didn't get the best from either one of us."

Tim's smile was halfhearted. His voice sounded strained. "Come to any conclusions, Lindsay?"

She closed her eyes and kept them shut for several seconds. She still didn't know what she was going to say. "Yes, I've decided that it's probably a terrible idea for us to make love, but . . ."

He tipped her face up and stared deeply into her eyes. "I love that 'but,'" he muttered. "Tell me more."

"But we're probably going to anyway, so why do I keep fighting it?" Now that she'd said the words, they sounded right.

"Thank God!"

His arms tightened around her. He bent his head to nuzzle her neck. His breath was warm and his words, murmured against her skin—"Lindsay, love, you don't know how I feel"—seemed the sweetest words that she had ever heard.

His lips, warm and soft, moved up her neck and captured her earlobe. As his teeth gently raked her flesh, all the desire that had been brought to life last night, blossomed within her.

She shifted on Tim's lap, feeling him swelling beneath her, and angled her face to invite his kiss. He pressed his mouth hungrily on hers, his tongue invading deeply. He lifted one of his hands; she could feel it move and felt slightly disappointed when it brushed past her breast. But then, while her tongue danced with his, creating an ever-building drunkenness of her senses, she felt his hand in her hair. Hairpins dropped onto the table and the floor.

When she could feel the coil of hair loosen, she leaned back and gave her head a shake. Her hair swirled around her shoulders. She had never felt so free, so wild, so passionate. . . .

For a moment she worried about perhaps being *too* passionate, *too* hungry. There wasn't a thing she could do about it. There would be no holding back. But what if Tim didn't like it . . . ?

That unpleasant notion fizzled away as Tim picked up a strand of her hair and brought it to her lips. "Like silk, Lindsay. I love your hair."

"And I love yours," she said, threading her fingers into the crisp locks at his temples, all the while pressing kisses to his forehead, his cheeks, and, at last again, his mouth.

Tim made a sound—the same low moan of need that had stopped her the night before. But this time it spurred her on to kiss him more deeply, to become the aggressor, with darting thrusts of her tongue.

Tim's hand went to the top button of her blouse and he tugged her shirttails free of the waistband of her slacks. His palm smoothed up her midriff. Then he fitted his hand around her breast and teased her nipple with his thumb. Even through her bra, the sensation was exquisite torment.

She wanted more—and less. More contact of skin to skin, and nowhere near so many clothes—for both of them.

"Tim," she said breathlessly, "why are we doing this in a kitchen chair, when there are perfectly good beds upstairs?"

He let out a delighted laugh. "Beats me."

They climbed the stairs hanging on to each other, touching all the way. Lindsay couldn't possibly have counted steps this time; she was too engrossed in getting a head start on things by undoing the buttons on Tim's shirt. She was working on his belt buckle when they reached the landing. There he hesitated for a moment. "Your place or mine?"

"Mine," Lindsay gasped. "The bed's bigger."

In her room, still half-clinging to Tim, she caught sight of the pair of them in the mirror over the dresser. Her hair was wild, tumbling helter-skelter around her shoulders. Tim had been busy with her clothing during the trek upstairs. So there were the two of them—

shirts undone, shirttails hanging out, the end of Tim's belt dangling free, and Lindsay's slacks already unbuttoned, half unzipped and starting to slide down her hips.

"What?" Tim asked. Then he followed the direction of her gaze and let out a short gust of laughter.

"Aren't we a sight?"

"A beautiful sight—at least, *you* are," he said fervently.

And then his hands were on her, completing the work of disrobing her that he'd already begun. She helped him rid her of her blouse and slacks and shoes. And somehow she managed to get his shirt off, too. But when his hands went around behind her and he cleverly managed to undo the clasp of her bra with hardly any fumbling, she just stood there, reveling in his touch, though unable to banish completely the perennial worry of women: *Will he find me good to look at?*

That question was answered immediately. As he bared her breasts, Tim sucked in his breath, a harsh sound that was the greatest compliment Lindsay had ever heard. He lifted his hands to cover them, fondling and stroking, then took her nipples between thumb and forefinger and lightly pinched.

This new sensation, when she was already highly aroused, sent shafts of passion directly to her center. Shameless, she reached out and pressed her palm to the front of his trousers. He was fully erect, straining against the placket of his trousers . . . and large. Her hands trembled, hurrying as she moved to undo the button at his waistband.

As she reached, he did, too, into his pocket. He pulled out a foil-wrapped packet and started to put it discreetly on the nightstand next to the bed.

Lindsay stopped him with a gesture. Despite the raggedness of her breathing, she managed to say, "I'm glad you're prepared, Tim. I . . . thought about it, but I didn't do anything."

He grinned and held up the wrapped condom. "This represents a lightning trip out of the office at lunchtime today. Just for the record, Lindsay, I haven't needed to carry any of those around for a heck of a long time."

"You were that certain what my decision would be?"

Emotion rippled over his expressive features. "Not certain at all." He dropped the packet onto the night table. "It was hope, love, that sent me on that errand. Not certainty."

And then he swiftly stepped out of his remaining clothing. Naked, he embraced her. The roughness of his chest hair teased her breasts. His arousal pressed against her belly. She wanted him so much that she was beyond thought, beyond speech. She clung to him, panting, as he eased her onto the bed and stretched out beside her.

He bent his head and took her nipple into his mouth. His tongue swirled circles around it as one of his hands slid down her midriff and her belly. His fingers toyed briefly in the soft thatch of hair between her thighs. Then, with one finger he found the special spot and Lindsay cried aloud. It was building too fast, with his mouth on her breast and his hand moving, moving. She wanted to give him pleasure too, before—

She exploded in an exquisite, shattering climax. He held her and caressed her—hips, thighs, shoulders— avoiding the most sensitive places as she gradually recaptured the pieces of her scattered self.

When she could speak again, she muttered against Tim's shoulder, "I was afraid that would happen."

"What?" He peered curiously at her. "I couldn't hear you, love."

"I said that I was afraid that would happen," she said ruefully. "It's been a long time, Tim. I'm sorry."

"Sorry? What on earth for? I loved it." He twisted around and gently kissed her lips. "I'll bet you're capable of more tonight. Aren't you, Lindsay?"

She nodded shyly. "I wouldn't be surprised."

"Then you're going to have more. Lots more."

His hands touched her, seeking out all the places where she was most sensitive, most alive. This time, she was able to think of Tim's pleasure, too. She touched and kissed, taking great delight in the drugged look she was able to bring to his face, in the deep groan he let out when she circled his erection with her hand and caressed him with long, firm strokes.

Before she would have thought it possible, renewed passion had gathered in her lower body, hot and demanding. She opened her knees and Tim poised himself over her. With joy and spiraling excitement, she felt his first probing touch. He froze, his face darkening. She didn't have to ask why when he turned away from her and reached for the packet he'd left on the nightstand. He'd almost forgotten, she realized, and she hadn't thought about it at all. *Very smart, Lindsay.*

And then he was over her again and her dismay vanished as she felt him entering her, filling all the hollow places, not only in her body, but in her heart.

He thrust deeply, then angled his shoulders so he could look down at the joining of their bodies. His eyes were heavy lidded, his firm mouth a little slack with passion. "Look at us, Lindsay. It's . . . it's wonderful."

She wouldn't have thought she would find it all that appealing, but when she lifted her head to watch him sliding in and out of her, a new surge of excitement took her by surprise. "You're right," she gasped, letting her head drop back against the pillow. "It's beautiful."

"*You*'re beautiful!" he insisted. Then all his muscles tensed and he picked up his pace.

Lindsay centered herself on Tim's deep, penetrating strokes. Her hips moved, striving with him until she hit a peak where she could no longer breathe and a storm of pleasure tossed her toward release. At her internal rippling, Tim tensed, pushed deeply into her, and shuddered, letting out a hoarse cry.

Then he was beside her, cradling her in his arms and murmuring words of praise and delight that were only sweeter for being half incoherent.

A minute later, or an hour—Lindsay wasn't certain which—she felt his hand on her hipbone. She opened her eyes to find him gazing at her, his expression tender. "That was wonderful, Lindsay. Much more so than I dreamed."

"For me, too." She curled a little closer to him. "I feel so at peace, Tim."

A wicked sparkle ignited in his eyes. "Only temporarily, love." His touch turned into a caress, his hand sliding down her thigh. "There's more for you tonight, you know."

She opened her eyes wide. "Oh, Tim. I don't *think* so."

"*I* do," he said firmly, and proceeded to demonstrate that he was right.

6

LINDSAY SWAM SLOWLY up from the depths of sleep, unwilling to let go of the erotic dream she'd had. Even now, there was a warmth and coziness to the bed, a comfort and contentment that must be left over from...

Her eyelids lifted and she found herself staring at a muscular, tanned arm. Reality popped back into focus. It hadn't been a dream. She and Tim had made love to each other for most of the night. They had made love with passion and tenderness, with humor and delight.

From the angle of the sunlight slanting through the blinds she realized that they had also slept away most of the morning.

The arm moved and Lindsay raised her gaze slowly to Tim's face. His eyes were open; his lips curved in a lazy smile as he turned his head to look at her.

Her heart seemed to skip a beat as she focused on his face. Making love with Tim had been the most fulfilling experience Lindsay had ever known. Her mind refused to just relax and enjoy the morning-after contentment. It had to ask questions. How would it be between them today? Tomorrow? The next day?

Would it be easy, comfortable? Or would there be remnants of the awkwardness they had experienced at work yesterday?

And what would it be like for them to be both partners in business and lovers at home? Could they keep the parameters of their two different relationships clear, without letting any debris from one spill over into the other?

She couldn't bear to ask herself what would happen to their work relationship when, given the age difference between them, their romantic relationship ended. That question went onto a little shelf of its own, shrouded in the dark.

Tim shifted, putting his arm around her and pulling her closer so her head nestled against his chest. "How are you feeling this morning, sweetheart? Any regrets?"

"Not regrets, exactly. Concerns, I guess you'd call them."

"Tell me."

She sighed. "Nothing new, Tim. How this will affect our working together is the main one, I guess."

He squeezed her reassuringly. "As long as we keep talking honestly, Lindsay. I'm sure it'll—"

He broke off at the sound of a door slamming downstairs. The front door. Lindsay recognized its solid, reverberant *thunk*. She lifted her head. "Who—"

A calling voice immediately answered her question. "Hey, Mom! Tim! Anybody home?"

Lindsay bolted up, wrenching free of Tim's encircling arm. "It's Dina," she whispered. "Oh, Lord in heaven!"

Tim reached out and touched Lindsay's shoulder. "Calm down, sweetheart," he said soothingly. "You'd better holler and let her know you're here. And then we can figure out how we're going to handle this."

Lindsay nodded. She had to swallow *and* clear her throat before calling loudly, "I'll be down in a minute, hon. Start some coffee going, okay?"

As Dina's "Okay" floated up the stairs, Lindsay was mostly hearing what Tim had said: "...how we're going to handle this." It was his "we" that got her. She'd been in a "we" with Tim, in business. And now, that same "we" was going to decide—

What in heaven's name were they going to do about Dina?

She must have voiced part of that thought aloud, because Tim said, keeping his voice low, "The way I see it, we've got a couple of options. I can sneak back to the guest room while you're downstairs, and while she's here, we'll pretend."

She swung her legs over the side of the bed. She wasn't wearing a stitch. Her instinct—or was it pure cowardice?—was to agree that pretending was the only possible way to handle the situation. But before she could say so, Tim went on, "This is your house and Dina's your kid, so if that's how you want to do it, I'll go along with it. However..."

She felt the mattress dip as he moved across the bed toward her. He wrapped his arms around her from behind. His voice was a murmur in her ear. "Seems to me it might be just as well to level with Dina. I mean, I'm going to be here next week and the week after that. At least, I hope I am." He chuckled. "You're not the kind of lady to seduce me and then toss me aside after only one night, are you?"

Despite her concern, Lindsay giggled. "*Me* seduce *you?*" she whispered indignantly. "Is that what happened?"

"Absolutely." He held her a little more tightly and Lindsay relaxed a fraction.

"Okay," she said. "I agree. I guess there's really no choice but to be up-front with Dina. I just don't know how I'm going to tell her." Another giggle burst out of her. She ought not to feel this good, under the circumstances. She thought it must be a sense of well-being so deep and solid that even her worry about how Dina would react could not entirely quell it. "I suppose we could just both wander down to the kitchen stark-naked," she whispered. "Dina's a smart kid. If we did that, she'd figure it out."

She felt Tim's exaggerated shudder. "I'm sure we can think of something better than that."

Lindsay sighed. "I'll just . . . tell her." But with what words, she had no idea.

And she still had no idea when, five minutes later, having brushed her teeth and hair, and pulled on her favorite beige caftan, she entered the kitchen to find the coffee brewing and her daughter sitting at the kitchen table, turning the pages of the newspaper. "Hi, honey," Lindsay said. "This is a pleasant surprise."

"Hi, Mom." Dina laughed at a comic strip, then glanced up at her mother. "I remembered this morning that Aunt Joanne's benefit was today, so I decided on the spur of the moment to drive down." Her eyes narrowed as she looked up at Lindsay. "Boy, you sure slept in this morning. Do you know it's nearly eleven?" She laughed. "Tim must have you indulging in riotous living. I've never known you to stay in bed so late."

Lindsay mumbled something. The words still wouldn't come that would let her inform her daughter that she was . . . Was what? That was the first problem. Having an affair? But could you even use that term to refer to one night of lovemaking, however rapturous? Although Tim *had* made it clear that he wanted more, expected more, than a proverbial one-night stand.

She could, she supposed, tell Dina that she and Tim were "involved." That word seemed accurate and relatively inoffensive. So one problem was solved. But Tim himself was the other major difficulty. Or rather, his age was.

Dina was exactly as much younger than Tim as Tim was younger than Lindsay. Dina had pulled down good grades in math in high school; she'd figure that one out. And by the standards of the world, it would have been more suitable for Tim and Dina to be romantically involved than Tim and Dina's *mother*.

"Mom. Hey, Mom!" Dina was waving her hand back and forth in front of Lindsay's face. "What's the matter? You've hardly said a word. And where's Tim? I saw his car out front. Is he sleeping in, too?" Her gaze went to the center of the kitchen table, where Lindsay saw, with a cold wave of horror passing through her, a neat pile of hairpins—the ones Tim had removed from her hair last night while he was kissing her.

Additional clues to what had happened sat on the counter, where the lid of the pizza box was open, giving a clear view of the cold, unappetizing leftovers—the slices not wrapped up in foil or put in the refrigerator, as Lindsay would have done, had her mind and body not been occupied with more important matters.

Thank heaven, she thought, that all their actual undressing of each other had taken place upstairs!

Dina picked up a hairpin and held it up. "What did you do, Mom? Let your hair down last night?" She giggled at her own joke. "I found these all over the floor. Boy, you guys must have had some party!"

Lindsay responded with a garbled "Mmbl" and felt a wave of heat rise in her cheeks. She pulled out a kitchen chair and sat down.

"Mom?" Dina said uncertainly, gazing at Lindsay's face. Her laughter had fled; on her piquant face was a combination of astonishment and dismay.

Lindsay took a deep breath. "Dina, honey, there's something I need to talk to you about. It's about me and Tim."

"You and Tim . . ." Understanding dawned in Dina's eyes. She held up her hand, her first finger crossed over the second, and said slowly, "You mean, as in *you* and *Tim?*"

She shook her head and Lindsay leaned over to anxiously cover her daughter's hand with her own. "I know it must be a bit surprising. I mean, it was a surprise to me, too. I had no idea that he felt . . . that *I* felt . . ." She realized that whereas before she had been virtually mute, now she was babbling. "I know he's a lot younger than me, and that must be a little bit shocking to you, Dina. But we do know each other pretty well, from working together, so it's not as if we're strangers and—"

"Hold on, Mom." Dina emitted a strained little laugh. "You don't really owe me any explanations. Tim's a great guy. I don't know . . . I just never thought of you and him that way. It's just . . . a little weird, I guess. But okay . . . I think."

Despite Dina's many qualifications, what Lindsay felt was overwhelming relief. "Thanks, honey. I was hoping you wouldn't be *too* upset."

Dina gave her mother's hand a reassuring squeeze. Then she took her hand away. "Oh, brother! And I was the one who suggested Tim stay here. How convenient! You must have thought I was really naive!"

"No, no. It wasn't like that," Lindsay said hurriedly. The last thing she wanted was for her daughter to think she'd been lied to, even by omission. "Tim and I *really were* just friends before." She paused. If she owed honesty to Tim, she owed it just as much to her daughter. "Well, that's not *quite* right. The truth is, I've been attracted to him for a long time. And he says he's felt the same way about me. But neither of us had said or done anything about it until after he moved in here."

"Oh, boy." Dina ignored all but the latter part of Lindsay's explanation. "So you two have been together less than a week and the kid shows up without warning." She expelled a gust of air. "Perfect!"

Something in Lindsay's face must have given her away, because Dina peered closely at her. "A *lot* less than a week, wasn't it?"

Lindsay nodded slowly.

"Last night?" Dina squeaked.

"It's okay, hon," Lindsay started to assure her, but Dina slapped her forehead with her hand. "That does it! I'm getting out of here."

"Dina, no! Wait! I don't *want* you to leave."

"You may not, but I'll bet Tim does."

"You lose *that* bet," spoke Tim's voice from the doorway.

IT WAS OKAY, Lindsay thought an hour later. Somehow, Tim had managed to reassure Dina that she wasn't, as Dina had put it, a third wheel. Dina had been convinced to stay, and all three had breakfasted together—Tim joking with Dina in a manner designed to put her at her ease.

There still might be some awkwardnesses, but the worst of it was over.

Now Dina was in her room, getting in a little studying before the three of them left for Joanne's benefit.

Lindsay herself had just finished showering and dressing and was standing in the bathroom, putting her hair up.

And Tim? She wasn't sure where Tim was, though she could somehow feel his presence in the house. Weird—that although she couldn't hear any of his sounds, she knew he was here. With a pang of dismay, Lindsay realized that Tim had already become so integral a part of her life, the house would feel empty without him.

She stuck the last of the pins into her chignon just as she heard a light tap on her bedroom door. "Come in," she called, and emerged from the bathroom just in time to greet Tim as he entered the room. "Hi, there! What have you been up to?"

He laughed. "Fixing things."

"What?"

"Seeing Dina reminded me I was supposed to be taking care of her 'poor old decrepit mother' by doing a few chores around here."

"You didn't have to do that."

"I know. But I wanted to. It didn't amount to much, anyway. Just a few washers in faucets and some oil on the hinges of the back door."

Tim grinned. He had thoroughly enjoyed himself. Wielding the wrench he had found in the garage, he had felt at home in a way he had never felt in his condo. And that was only the mildest of the emotions he'd experienced this morning. More important was his relief that Dina didn't seem to be too upset, plus a genuine liking for her.

He'd never before felt anything remotely like what he was feeling for Lindsay. Certainly not with any of the

Bambis. Not even in college when he'd briefly considered himself to be in love.

This was different—more solidly anchored in genuine caring for Lindsay as a person. This *was* love and he knew it. Just looking at her now, he felt things too powerful to put into words. He would try to tell her. Not now, but soon . . .

He looked at her and opened his arms. "Come here, woman. You're much too far away!"

She walked straight into his arms. "You were great with Dina," she said, snuggling against his chest.

"She's a terrific kid. She's going to be okay about you and me, isn't she?"

Lindsay nodded instead of speaking because she liked the sensation of rubbing her cheek against Tim's shoulder. He was wearing a crisp white shirt, pinstriped in maroon and navy, with a navy tie and navy slacks.

And beneath those slacks she could feel the evidence that the contact between them was having its effect. It was having an effect on her, too, which was rather amazing to Lindsay, considering how thoroughly satiated she'd been the night before. But already she felt little tinglings, frissons of sensation.

She tightened her hold on Tim, looked up at him and warned, "I'm not sure about tonight, Tim—whether we ought to share a room with Dina here. She might need some time to get used to the situation before we . . ."

"Rub it in?" Tim finished for her. "I agree. Let's play it by ear, though." His voice lowered and grew husky. "Now that I've found you, I don't want to lose you, not even for a single night—unless it absolutely *has* to be that way."

His words, his tone, made her feel breathless. "Tim..." she said, just because she wanted to speak his name.

He bent his head and kissed her, deeply, thoroughly. When it was over, his eyebrows danced. "There you go, woman—trying to seduce me again. And succeeding, may I add? Come on. Time for me to take you two 'girls' to Joanne's benefit."

A few moments later, Lindsay knocked on Dina's door. "Ready to go, hon?"

Dina popped out, dressed and ready. Mother and daughter reached the landing to find Tim downstairs, waiting by the front door. "My car?" he asked.

"Great!" Dina said enthusiastically. "Hey, Tim! Would you let me drive your car some time? I'm a good driver, honestly I am."

Tim looked over Dina's head. "Is she telling the truth... *Mom?*"

"She sure is. She's never even had a ticket."

Tim held his keys out to Dina. "Well, then, why don't you chauffeur your mom and me to the benefit?"

"All *right!*" Dina whooped and grabbed the keys as if afraid that if she hesitated, he might change his mind.

LINDSAY FOLDED HERSELF to climb into the back seat of Tim's sports car. His legs were too long to fit comfortably in the back, so she had volunteered. She didn't mind a bit. It was well worth a little folding to see Dina and Tim establishing a comfortable relationship with each other.

She was halfway in, her derriere protruding rather unaesthetically, she feared, when a thought struck her and she let out a muffled exclamation. How could she have forgotten until now that she had made a date with Adam Holloway for tonight?

If she hadn't remembered at all, wouldn't *that* have been cute?—the possibility of Adam showing up on her doorstep and her having to say something like "Oh, Adam, I think you've met my partner, Tim Reynolds, haven't you? Well, he's not just my partner. He's my lover now, and ..."

She backed hastily out of the car, bumping into Tim, who was holding the door for her. "What's the matter?" he asked, though he didn't seem to mind a bit having been bumped into since he was smiling.

"Uh ... I forgot something," she told him. "Back in a flash."

SHE WAS A LITTLE SORRY that Adam picked up, instead of his answering machine. After identifying herself, she said, "I'm really sorry, Adam, but I'm going to have to cancel our date tonight. Something's, uh ... come up."

"I'm sorry to hear that, Lindsay. I guess I can't complain too much about it since I had to cancel last time. How about next week sometime? Do you think—"

"No, Adam," she responded gently. "The truth is ... I've, well, gotten involved with someone." Convenient word, *involved*. She was glad she'd thought of it.

"Oh." He cleared his throat. "I'm glad for you, then, Lindsay."

"Thank you. So am I."

A very nice man, she reflected as she hurried out to the car where her daughter and her lover were waiting for her. But not the right man for her.

DINA PEERED curiously at Lindsay as she climbed into the back seat. "What was that about? Did you forget something?"

"Just something I had to take care of." She settled herself. Tim got into the front seat, then turned his head to look at her. His eyes met hers, and in them she read total understanding. She didn't know how he could have known what she'd had to do inside, but it was obvious he knew what *kind* of thing it was.

"All set?" he asked lightly as she pulled her seat belt across her body and snapped it.

"All set," she said firmly.

TIM WHISTLED through his teeth as Dina followed a Jaguar off the Bel Air street onto a private drive that bisected spacious grounds. He had very nicely, in Lindsay's opinion, not shown any signs of tension over Dina driving his car, even on the twisting road that climbed the hills between the valley and the west-side area of L.A. "Pretty snazzy place!" he exclaimed.

Before them, as they moved slowly in the line of cars up the drive, was a flagstone mansion. Spread out in front of the house was a miniature fairground, with booths and tents set up in parallel rows. A small ferris wheel and a merry-go-round occupied a stretch of lawn off to the left, while cars were being directed to a paved parking area in the back.

"It's hard to believe people really live like this," Lindsay observed.

Tim chuckled. "With a carnival in their front yards, you mean?"

She would have leaned forward to punch him lightly on the arm, but she wasn't sure if Dina was ready to see physical contact between them yet, even of such an innocuous kind. "That's not what I meant," she protested with a smile for Tim.

"It *is* pretty elaborate," he said as they inched slowly past tennis courts and a gigantic pool.

At the end of the long driveway they were directed into a parking slot by a red-jacketed attendant. The three of them got out of the car, Dina conscientiously handing the keys to Tim, then joined the stream of people moving toward the main area of booths and tents.

The boxy plywood booths were elaborately trimmed with colorful paper streamers, artificial flowers and bright splashes of paint of every conceivable color. Huge signs, deftly hand-painted with an adman's knack of luring customers, stretched across the front of each. Hungry? the nearest booth inquired. Here's The Place!

Beyond were more food booths, games and displays. Lots to look at, lots to do—even apart from the rides set up a short distance away.

Tim surveyed the scene, then said, "Well, ladies, what shall we do first? I assume the object is for us to spend as much money as we can possibly afford."

"You got it," Lindsay replied. "All in the name of a good cause, of course."

Jerking his head at a nearby booth that invited patrons to throw softballs at a row of bowling pins, Tim suggested, "Well, I could try to win you two lovelies one of those pink teddy bears. That's an activity virtually guaranteed to part me from my loose change."

"You're not Dead-Eye Dick? Is that what you're saying?" Lindsay asked curiously. So there were *some* things she didn't know about him—and what fun it was going to be to find out!

"I'm terrible," he said cheerfully. "Track was my sport in high school. I can run and jump okay, but my aim isn't the greatest."

She cast a sideways glance at him, thinking how unusual Tim was. Most men claimed all kinds of physical prowess—whether they possessed it or not—excusing failure on the grounds of having an off day, or for some other pretentious reason.

Tim was amply blessed with the only kind of physical prowess that concerned her. She cast him an oblique glance. Images welled up in her: Tim's hands on her breasts, her thighs; his tongue filling her mouth. She felt a wash of heat and desire, and wondered if she would ever, no matter how long they were together, have enough of Tim.

"Maybe I'd better be the one to try to win the teddy bear, then," Dina suggested. "I've got great aim."

"It's true, she does," Lindsay said, as if Tim had challenged her daughter's claim.

"I'll give it a—" Dina broke off. "That's Marcy Peters!" she exclaimed, peering through the crowd toward a booth near the end of the row. "I haven't seen her since graduation."

Lindsay recalled that Dina and Marcy had been fairly good friends in high school. Marcy had gone east to school.

"What's she doing here? She's supposed to be at Wellesley," Dina murmured. "I've got to go talk to her. I'll catch up with you guys later." She darted a teasing glance at Tim. "If Mom is dying to have a pink teddy bear, I guess it's up to you." She ran off through the crowd, already calling, "Marcy! Hey, Marcy!"

"Do you want a pink teddy bear?" Tim asked.

"Not particularly."

"Let's just wander, then, shall we?" He paused, then added thoughtfully, "Or should we go check in with Joanne first, let her know we're here? After all, she is our main reason for coming."

"I guess we should." Lindsay wasn't certain yet how much she'd tell Joanne—or whether she'd tell her anything at all about her and Tim. Eventually she'd want to clue her best friend in, but for now, it was still new and private—a precious gift that she'd prefer to savor for a little while, like a miser gloating over secret treasure.

Tim peered over the crowd, then pointed. "There's her tent."

Lindsay saw a huge purple banner stretched between two poles. Madam Mysteria Knows All, Tells All, it read.

They turned in that direction and moved a few steps. As they veered to avoid a mother pushing a toddler in a stroller, Tim's right hand brushed Lindsay's left. He took her hand, lacing his fingers through hers.

Lindsay tensed. There was something so incontrovertible about holding hands. Anyone seeing them would know . . .

And would see what? A woman older than the man she was with? Would anyone even be able to tell? She didn't know if their age difference was visible or not. And what difference did it make, anyway? It wasn't as if she was a blue-haired dowager with a thirty-years-younger gigolo.

Tim watched the play of emotions on Lindsay's face, feeling both tenderness and concern. Though she had given him her body—and *how* she had given it: unstintingly, generously, passionately—in some respects she was still resisting their relationship. It was obvious in so many little things, like the way she had stiffened when he took her hand.

Why was it so complicated for her? To him it was simplicity itself. They were a couple now; and he wanted them to be the way couples were with each other, have everything that couples had. At last her hand relaxed within his, her fingers curling and clinging, and he felt a connection flow between them, so strong that he thought again: *Yes. This is love. The real thing. The "forever" kind.*

"TICKET?" It took Lindsay a moment to realize that the gray-haired woman controlling the flow of Madame Mysteria's customers was addressing her. The line waiting outside Joanne's tent had been a long one, but somehow, with Tim beside her, the time had seemed to fly.

She smiled up at Tim as she handed over the colored cardboard rectangle. He returned her smile. Then, just as the gray-haired attendant opened the tent flap for Lindsay to enter, he put his hand on the back of her neck and squeezed gently. For a moment, he gazed deeply into her eyes. "Hurry back," he said meaningfully, then pressed a quick kiss to her hair.

"I will," she assured him huskily, then turned to enter the tent—and saw Joanne seated inside, directly opposite the open tent flap. She was swathed in rainbow-colored layers of filmy cloth, a gaudy turban concealed her hair and—her wide eyes and open mouth gave ample evidence that she had seen Tim's intimate gestures.

So much for not telling Joanne right away about her new relationship with Tim....

Lindsay entered the tent and the flap closed behind her. Directly in front of her was a square table swathed in chiffon. Intricately festooned draperies disguised the tent's canvas walls. A small lamp in a corner provided the only light, but its dim yellow glow was sufficient for her to see the avid curiosity in Joanne's blue eyes.

Lindsay seated herself in the empty chair. "My reading?" she suggested.

Joanne leaned forward, resting her elbows on the table. "Reading, schmeading! What's with you and Tim?" Without warning, she snapped her fingers. "Before I forget . . . Dina came by to see me a little while ago. She said to tell you that she left with her friend, Marcy." Joanne eyed Lindsay. "She said you'd know who that was."

"Marcy Peters," Lindsay supplied.

"Whatever . . ." Joanne waved her hand dismissively. "Anyway, Marcy'll bring Dina home later. That's the message. *Now*, what about you and Tim?"

Lindsay decided to be stubborn. She crossed her arms over her chest. "You're Madame Mysteria. You tell me!"

Joanne grimaced. "You are the most maddening person, Lindsay Ames. You know you're going to tell me."

"What makes you so sure?"

Joanne cocked her head to one side. "Because I'm not letting you out of here until you do?" she said questioningly.

"Well, all right. But *after* I get my reading." Maybe the extra time would help her figure out how to explain to Joanne what had happened between her and Tim—which she wasn't altogether certain she understood herself.

But she wasn't given much time. Joanne gave her the tarot deck to hold while Lindsay thought of a question. The only truly meaningful question—what would happen with her and Tim's relationship—she didn't ask because her sensible side thought it already knew the answer. It couldn't last; not in the long term. Eventually Tim would get ready to marry and settle down. And then he'd think of children, of a life with someone, and he would realize he needed a woman younger than Lindsay—someone ready to start a family and be a lifelong partner.

But it might be quite some time before that happened, she hoped. All she could do was enjoy it while it lasted and pray that the disintegration, when it came, wouldn't hurt *too* badly.

She thought of some question that she forgot as soon as it was formulated, then watched with amusement as Joanne slapped down the cards at breakneck speed, then interpreted their meanings as if she were competing for a prize for speaking the greatest number of words in the shortest possible amount of time.

"Do it, don't do it. Who cares? It doesn't matter," Joanne finished. "That's it. I'm done." She gathered the cards back together, then slapped the deck down on the table and glared at Lindsay. "All right. Now, *speak!*"

Lindsay said basically the same things she'd said to Dina, except that she was encouraged to elaborate by Joanne's frequent utterances of "Uh-huh" and "Then, what happened?"

When she finished, Joanne wore a Cheshire-cat smile. "See! I told you you'd meet Mr. Right."

"Yes, you did. You just got the wrong Mr. Right, that's all." She sobered. "Only Tim's not really Mr. Right. Not for me."

"Why on earth not?"

"He *is* ten years younger than me."

"Oh, pooh!" Joanne said with an airy wave of her hand. "You don't exactly have one foot in the grave, you know. I'm really happy for you, kiddo. You know that?" Before Lindsay could respond, Joanne blurted, "Oh, shoot!"

"What?" Lindsay asked, startled.

"Nothing."

"Come on, Joanne. What is it?"

"It's not important, really. I just realized we won't be having lunch tomorrow, will we? Don't worry about it, though," she went on brightly. "I bet April Maddox is free." She rolled her eyes. "She's *always* free, poor thing."

Lindsay thought quickly. Joanne had just raised a significant issue, one that she and Tim hadn't had time to discuss—the extent to which they would still act independently, having their own activities, seeing their own, separate friends.

"So, you're throwing me over for April Maddox, are you?" Lindsay jokingly accused Joanne. "A fine friend you are."

Joanne blinked. "I just assumed—"

"Stop assuming," Lindsay told her. "Lunch tomorrow. Twelve o'clock at Berton's, just as we planned."

TIM WAS NEXT in line as Lindsay emerged from Madame Mysteria's tent. "How'd it go?" he asked, and put his hand on her waist, just because they'd been separated for nearly half an hour and he needed to touch her.

She glanced up at the banner over the tent. "That sign's a lie. She doesn't 'tell all,' she gets other people to do it." She laughed at the expression on Tim's face.

"Don't worry. I don't share the really personal stuff, not even with Joanne."

"I didn't think you did," he assured her.

The gray-haired ticket taker cleared her throat meaningfully and Tim said, "Guess I'd better get in there or I'll lose my turn."

FIFTEEN MINUTES LATER, he emerged from the tent and looked around for Lindsay. He couldn't see her anywhere and though he ached for the sight of her, for her scent and softness, for her wonderful, low voice, her radiant smile, he was just as glad to have a moment to settle into the decision he'd made while Joanne was reading the cards.

She'd told him to hold the pack and think of a question he wanted answered. The question that had popped into his mind had startled him a bit, but there it was, emblazoned in his mind in letters larger than those on Madame Mysteria's banner: How soon should he ask Lindsay to marry him?

Funny, he thought now, that his question hadn't been *if* he should propose, just *when*.

Naturally he hadn't spoken his question aloud. And he'd answered it himself, without the help of the cards or Madame Mysteria. It was a matter of logic, really. He'd promised Lindsay total honesty. And now that he knew with a deep, inner certainty that what he wanted was to marry her, it would be less than honest if he didn't tell her so.

Sober counsel would insist that it was too soon; that he and Lindsay had been together, in the deepest, truest sense of the word, only since last night. But that didn't matter. He knew everything he needed to know about her.

He *knew*, so what was the point of waiting? Why not get on with it. There were, after all, things they'd need to work out.

7

LINDSAY SAT on the edge of the bed without a stitch of clothing on. Looking up, she inhaled sharply at the sight of Tim's equally naked body. Last night, she'd been too intoxicated with desire to look at him as closely as she might have. Now she noticed that the fine brown hair covering his chest tapered, lower down, to a narrow line that drew the eye over a flat, hard belly to the nest of hair with its proud centerpiece.

She returned her gaze to his face and smiled. "Call me a terrible mother, but I'm not one bit sorry Dina decided to spend the night at Marcy Peters's house."

Tim stepped forward, putting himself in reach of Lindsay's hands. "You're not a terrible mother." He grinned. "You've obviously raised an extremely thoughtful and tactful daughter."

"Remind me to thank her one day," Lindsay murmured. But probably not tomorrow.

To thank her for absenting herself so Lindsay and Tim could sleep together without worrying about Dina's feelings would be a little too . . . racy. Five years from now, or ten, she might be able to say something like that and Dina would laugh. But not yet.

Lindsay was glad that when Dina had called to inform her of the "slumber party" at Marcy Peters's, as she'd ironically referred to it, she had acquiesced readily to her mother's suggestion that they have a late breakfast together the following day.

That late breakfast would be followed in short order by lunch with Joanne—not exactly Lindsay's idea of an ideal eating schedule. But both get-togethers were necessary, in her opinion, to the care and feeding of two relationships that were important to her.

When she had mentioned her plans to Tim, he had said only that he was sorry they couldn't spend the whole day together, but of course she should go ahead. He'd probably play racquetball with his friend Rafe Kramer.

So much for her worries about how they would handle the separate friendships in their lives. If only her other worries proved to be as insubstantial as that one....

But there seemed absolutely nothing to worry about at the moment. As soon as they had learned that Dina wouldn't be coming home tonight, Lindsay and Tim had fixed their gazes on each other. "Great minds," she had murmured.

"Definitely thinking alike," Tim had finished. He'd grabbed her hand and, as one, they had raced up the stairs.

Now, already thoroughly aroused by the kisses and caresses she and Tim had shared as they "helped" each other to undress, she leaned forward to touch her lips to the tip of Tim's erection. Her hands went around behind him, first testing the shape of his buttocks with her palms, then kneading deeply.

"Oh, Lord in heaven, Lindsay," he muttered. "What you're doing is . . . wonderful."

It pleased her beyond measure that she could make him shudder with pleasure; she was already learning what he particularly liked, and each groan she man-

'aged to elicit from him made her own excitement spiral
to a higher level.

Tim's hands on her breasts as she continued to touch
and caress him soon made her feel as if she would jump
right out of her skin if she couldn't feel him inside her.
She lay back on the bed, pulling Tim with her. He
moved over her, but did not poise himself for entry.
"My turn to do wonderful things to you," he said.

Wonderful was far too mild a word, Lindsay discovered a few moments later. He had begun with the hollow at the base of her throat and, inching his way down
the bed, left a trail of blazing kisses on her breasts, her
belly, her thighs.

Then he parted her soft, damp triangle of hair and
drew a gently exploring fingertip down her slippery
crevice, to position his finger at her opening. As he slid
his finger delicately into her, his lips found the tiny bud
of pleasure between her folds of flesh and the tip of his
tongue lightly prodded that sensitive nub. She began
to feel as if it were glowing—a fiery coal radiating its
heat all the way to the top of her head and the tips of
her toes.

Tim went on, and his lovemaking was delicate and
controlled, as if her body were a fine piece of precision
machinery whose every working part he thoroughly
understood. But there was nothing refined about the
explosion of pleasure he brought her to. She cried
aloud, her entire body shuddering as internal spasms
buffeted her.

He left her for an instant, but before the sensations
had completely receded, he was back with her, poised
over her. Then he sheathed himself deep within her.
Supporting his weight on his hands, he remained mo-
tionless, just . . . filling her.

Still without moving his lower body, he shifted the angle of his shoulders and bent his head. The heat of his mouth on her breast, the rhythmical flicking of his tongue over her nipple and the sensation of him buried deep within her began to renew the heat and gathering tension in her lower body.

Only when she initiated movement with an involuntary lifting of her hips did Tim begin to move, with slow, deep thrusts that made her excitement built and build. Just as she could feel herself reaching the vortex that precedes release, his rhythm broke and the flurry of strokes that signaled his own climax propelled her over the edge into a place where nothing existed but her body's convulsive ecstasy.

When her mind returned her from that place, Tim was holding her and saying, "You, my sweet, are absolutely terrific in bed."

She liked his frankness and decided to return it with frankness of her own. "And you, sir, are extraordinary." She gazed at him with genuine admiration. That he could have managed, after the things she'd done to him earlier, to hold back long enough to bring her twice to climax struck her as a noteworthy feat. "Such control," she added. "Such consideration."

"That's not really it at all," he told her seriously. He trailed his hand down her bare arm. "It's actually pure selfishness, Lindsay. I get such pleasure from pleasing you that I'd like to do it over and over and over again."

Tim reprimanded himself, though he concealed it from Lindsay. Again tonight, he had caught himself on the verge of forgetting to use the condom he had placed on the nightstand. Perhaps he should warn her that she shouldn't altogether trust him; that at the moments of the most intense passion, she should check to make sure he wasn't about to do something that would be unfair to her. But putting the responsibility on her wasn't fair, either. . . .

He let the thought drift away; there was something else he had to say to her tonight. And, glancing over at her, seeing her eyes were heavy lidded, he'd better say it soon or he'd find himself only a distant voice in her dreams.

"Lindsay? Don't go to sleep quite yet. Okay? I want to talk to you."

She opened her eyes. She hadn't really been on the verge of sleep, just drifting in a profound contentment. "Sure," she said, and snuggled a little closer to him.

"Lindsay. . ." To her, his voice turned her name into a caress. "I wanted to wait until now, so you'd know I wasn't just saying this in the throes of passion. I love you."

She froze. Her heart expanded until she thought it would explode through the walls of her chest—only to collapse into a cold, hard knot.

When the person who is speaking is one you care about, "I love you" is a wonderful thing to hear; but only if you believe it to be true. And Lindsay simply couldn't believe it. Tim couldn't really mean those words—couldn't say them and *know* he meant them. It was too soon for such feelings. It was impetuous. Even immature. Love had to grow, step by step, over a very long time.

She put her fingertip to Tim's lips to silence him before he said more. "No. Please, Tim. Don't. It's too soon."

He caught her wrist. "It's *not* too soon. Not for me. I know how I feel."

But despite his protest, Tim could see he wasn't getting through to her, that she didn't believe him. If he was smart, he'd shut up and keep his emotions to himself until she was ready to hear. But he *did* know and he had to go on. He tightened his hold on her, for fear she might literally jump up and run away. "Let me tell you how certain I am of how I feel. I want to marry you, Lindsay. I'd marry you tomorrow if you'd say yes."

Lindsay shut her eyes. *Oh, Tim,* she thought sadly. *Don't do this. Don't shake my conception of you. Don't make me feel as if I have to protect you from yourself.*

Tim studied her face; her eyes were squinched up, as if against a too-bright light. She wasn't ready. She didn't love him . . . yet. For a moment, a cold terror overtook him, a fear that maybe she never would.

But he couldn't let himself believe that. Very well, then, he thought, he'd *make* her love him.

He loosened his grip and slid a gentle caress down her shoulder. "Too soon for that, huh?" he said, determinedly keeping his voice light.

"*Much* too soon," she answered forcefully. Marriage. It was too impossible an idea to take seriously. He was just caught up in the newness, the excitement of the first few days of a love affair. It was just fortunate, she reflected, that she was older, wiser, steadier. Another woman might actually have believed that he knew what he was saying and meant it.

"We'll leave it for now, then, Lindsay," he told her.

She heard the disappointment in his voice and stroked his arm consolingly, thinking: *One day he'll thank me.*

JOANNE ARCHED curious brows at Lindsay. "You're not eating much. Love got your appetite?"

"No." Lindsay smiled. "Breakfast did me in. Dina and I just got through eating about an hour ago."

Joanne rocked back in her chair. "And you didn't cancel lunch with me? You're a good friend, Lindsay Ames."

"And so are you to me."

"Well, I've never eaten two meals right together for your sake. Though there was that time in high school when I got rid of Kenny Cleveland for you. Remember?"

Lindsay grimaced. "Yeah, by telling him I was in love with that dumb big captain of the football team. What was his name?"

"Rod..." Joanne giggled. "How appropriate! Rod Bellows, I think."

"Right. And then *he* was after me for months."

"It was still an improvement over Kenny Cleveland," Joanne insisted. "At least, Rod Bellows didn't serenade you with his clarinet—"

"He couldn't play the clarinet."

"Or send you poems," Joanne went on, undaunted.

"Rod Bellows didn't know how to write."

"Well, it was the principle of the thing." Joanne lifted her fork. "If you're not going to eat your salad, can I sample? I won this lunch fair and square, and I intend to enjoy it."

"Sure. Help yourself." Lindsay pushed her nearly untouched plate toward Joanne.

Joanne chewed the bite she'd taken from Lindsay's plate. "Change-of-subject time. Does Dina know about you and Tim?"

Lindsay nodded.

"She have any problems with it?"

"Not really." Lindsay smiled ruefully. "She did ask me at breakfast if I thought Tim and I would get serious—'like, get married someday' were her exact words. And I thought she looked a bit relieved when I told her there was no chance of that. But she certainly doesn't hate him or anything."

Joanne speared a black olive from Lindsay's plate and popped it into her mouth. With a lump in her cheek, she said, "Who could hate Tim?"

"A kid who's having trouble with the idea of her mother as a sexual being, that's who," Lindsay responded. "And there's some of that going on with Dina, I think. But she's handling it okay. She'll be fine."

Joanne removed the olive pit from her mouth and put it on her plate. "You said there's no chance of you and Tim ever getting to the point of marriage. How can you be so sure?"

"It's obvious, isn't it?"

"Not to me."

Lindsay sighed. She didn't feel like going into the reasons why a long-term relationship with Tim was out of the question. But it wasn't in her to tell Joanne to butt out, so she explained what seemed so apparent to her.

"Well . . ." Joanne responded dubiously when she'd finished, "you have a point. Especially the part about having kids." She shuddered. "The thought of being pregnant again . . . I'd jump off a tall building first, and you know how scared I am of heights."

Lindsay blinked, surprised by the vehemence of Joanne's tone. She'd actually enjoyed being pregnant with Dina—until the last few weeks. It was the fact that, at less than three weeks from her fortieth birthday, she had already passed her best childbearing years. She was just plain *too old* to give Tim a brood of kids like the family he'd grown up in. You didn't go from two nights of love with a man, to marriage and children—no matter how impetuous your lover might be.

"You through eating?" Joanne asked.

"I sure am."

"Then, do you want to check out the little mall next door? Or do you have to get back?"

"I'm in no hurry. Tim's playing racquetball with a friend of his."

SINCE IT WAS SUNDAY, some of the shops in the mall were closed, but other enterprising merchants were open for business. Joanne steered Lindsay into a boutique. She swept between racks and carousels, then propelled Lindsay back outside with a muttered "Drab, drab, drab. Well, at least we checked it out."

"You may have checked it out," Lindsay said as they continued down the walk. "I didn't have a chance to see a thing."

"Trust me. I know my shopping." She came to an abrupt halt in front of a bookstore window. "Well, look at that!" Before Lindsay could figure out which book had caught Joanne's eye, the redhead had nipped inside.

Lindsay followed, browsing the magazine rack until Joanne had paid for her purchase. Outside, Joanne thrust the plastic bag into Lindsay's hands. "It's a present."

"What on earth?" Lindsay delved into the bag and drew out a hardback book: *Loving a Younger Man*, by Victoria Houston.

"Who knows?" Joanne winked. "It might be just what you need right now."

"HAPPY BIRTHDAY TO YOU, Happy Birthday to you...."

Lindsay tried to smile as she gazed at the cake their employees had smuggled into work today, without her knowledge. If she ever found out who was responsible for spreading the news that today was her birthday, she'd personally wring his or her neck.

Her neck, probably. Nancy was her leading suspect. Tim wasn't the guilty party; he knew she didn't want a fuss made and he wouldn't go against her wishes. He also knew that her desire for a fussless day was because of how ambivalent she felt about this birthday. The one thing he didn't know was that her negative feelings were largely because of her relationship with him. Prior to Tim's change of status in her life, she'd viewed the big four-O—the birthday that so many people thought of as an appalling milestone—with relative equanimity. Now, turning forty, especially since Tim would still be twenty-nine for another couple of months, made her feel not ten years older than he, but twenty.

She ought to reread the book Joanne had brought her to lift her spirits. The author of the book had met every fear with an answer, and that had helped. But not quite enough. And not *today*.

The raucous rendition of "Happy Birthday" ended. Thank heaven there was only one fat red candle on the cake. She blew it out, without actually making a wish, cut the cake and served it. When everyone had a piece, she said, "Thank you all so much. And though this has nothing to do with today being my birthday, I just want to say that you guys are all doing a terrific job. This is the smoothest tax season we've ever had."

Applause broke out, then died. Lindsay stood talking with her cake-eating staff. When the party showed signs of breaking up, she caught Tim's eye. He had

maintained an admirable discretion about their relationship. No furtive touches or intimate remarks at
work, except when they were alone in the privacy of his
office or hers.

He maintained decorum, waiting until they were in
the car and stopped at a red light several blocks from
the office to lean over and kiss her. "Happy Birthday,
birthday girl."

"You already wished me Happy Birthday this morning."

"And I'm going to go on doing it until the stroke of
midnight."

The red light changed to green. Only when he had
passed two more green lights did Lindsay realize he'd
driven past the turning to her house. "Where are we
going, Tim?"

"You'll see," he replied mysteriously.

AND SHE DID SEE, twenty minutes later when Tim
stopped the car at valet parking in front of a luxury
high-rise hotel. But she still didn't entirely catch on until they had walked through the lobby and were in the
elevator and Tim pulled a room key from his pocket.

She goggled at him. "You've already checked in?" She
squeezed his arm. "It's a nice idea, Tim, but I don't have
a toothbrush or a change of clothes for tomorrow or
anything."

He winked. "Yes, you do."

And so she did. "You're amazing," she said fervently, once they had entered the luxuriously appointed room. Work clothes for tomorrow hung in the
closet. Her cosmetic bag sat on the counter in the bathroom, which was equipped with both a phone and a
miniature TV.

She came back out of the bathroom, intending to thank Tim and compliment him on providing so well for her, but before she could speak, he opened a drawer in the dresser and pulled out a flat white box tied with red ribbon.

"Happy Birthday, Lindsay," he said and kissed her as he handed her the box.

She opened it, unfolded the tissue paper, and gasped with pleasure as she pulled out the slinkiest, sexiest, most elegant nightgown she had ever seen in her life. It was black and low-cut, with lace inserts, and the fabric was so slippery smooth, she knew it would feel like a caress on her skin.

She hugged Tim, then said suggestively, "Want me to model it?"

"Do I!" He glanced at his watch. "But not for another five minutes."

The reason became apparent when there was a knock at the door and Tim let two waiters in. One carried an ice bucket, in which sat a frosty bottle of champagne. The second waiter carried a huge display of long-stemmed red roses with frothy baby's breath adding frills of white to the vibrant crimson of the bouquet.

The two waiters sang "Happy Birthday" to her, slightly off-key, and were joined near the end by Tim's robust baritone.

"*Now* you can model the gown," he said when the door had closed behind the pair, "though about an hour from now, I'm going to insist you hide in the bathroom for a few minutes."

"What happens in an hour?" Lindsay asked curiously. At this point, she wouldn't have been too surprised if a brass band showed up to *play* "Happy Birthday" to her.

"Dinner," Tim replied succinctly.

In the bathroom, Lindsay slipped out of her dress, then, deciding she might as well go whole hog, turned on the bathtub taps.

In a moment there was a knock on the bathroom door. "You can't come in. I'm not ready yet," she protested.

"I'm not trying to peek," Tim said through the closed door. "I just thought if you're going to be in there for a while, you might want some champagne."

"You're a brilliant man, Tim Reynolds!" She opened the door and his hand came through, holding out a glass filled with golden bubbles.

Sipping champagne, Lindsay luxuriated in the hot bath, feeling pampered...feeling loved. And when she got out and slipped the sexy gown over her head, she smiled at her reflection in the steam-coated mirror. Her hair hung in a silky cloud around her shoulders; her skin was rosy from her bath; the gown made her full breasts look even fuller, her slim waist slimmer. How could she worry about turning forty when she looked like this? When she was treated like this by a man like Tim?

She opened the door a crack and announced, "Ta-da! Here I come!"

WHEN LINDSAY EMERGED from the bathroom, every muscle in his body stiffened. She was so incredibly beautiful, it almost hurt to look at her.

The past few weeks, his love for her had only increased and sometimes *that* was painful, too—a constant ache, as well as a constant joy. Every day he spent with her, he treasured; but every day made him want more—a lifetime of days; the commitment implied in marriage.

And she hadn't even said she loved him. Not once.

He burned to hear her say those words. Sometimes he was sure she loved him, and that if he pushed and pried and hinted, she would admit it. But he wanted her to *want* to say the three magic words, not be forced into saying them.

He had also known she was bothered by turning forty, though he saw absolutely no reason why she should feel that way. He had hoped a little special treatment would reassure her. But he hadn't expected that seeing her like this would make him feel totally undone by love and longing.

He reached for the phone. Lindsay looked a bit disappointed. "You're making a call?"

He shook his head and his voice emerged thick with emotion. "Just postponing dinner."

The gown did feel like a caress on Lindsay's skin, silky and sensual. But Tim's hands as he touched her through the gown, beneath the gown, and in places the gown did not cover, made her blaze with fever.

Meanwhile she slowly and lovingly began to remove his clothes, smoothing her palms over his hair-roughened chest, teasing his flat, male nipples with her tongue. Then, after his briefs had followed his trousers onto the floor, she caressed the parts of him that those garments had covered.

Naked, he looked down at her. "You look absolutely beautiful in that gown, Lindsay, but I'm sorry...it's got to go."

He made a sensual dance of its removal, sliding the straps down her shoulders, kissing her breasts as soon as they were bared, following the path of the fabric's descent down her body with his hands and mouth.

As he straightened and pulled her hard against him, Lindsay felt more aroused than ever in her life. She was vaguely aware of being a creature of the moon, subject to its cycles. Whenever she was midmonth, as she was now, she had the potential to be at her most sensual. Tim's care, his tenderness—not to mention his potent physical appeal—had brought her excitement to a level of intensity she had only dimly guessed might be possible for her.

Tim eased her down onto the bed, then lay beside her. With one hand, he reached for the glass of champagne he'd abandoned on the nightstand. With his fingertips, he dribbled the still-fizzy liquid onto her breast.

It was cool enough that the contrast to her heated skin gave her an unexpected sensual shock. Tim leaned over, and with long, slow strokes of his tongue, licked off the champagne. Her other breast got the same treatment, and by the time he had finished, her skin felt as if it were giving off waves of radiant heat. Her breasts felt swollen, the nipples like burning pebbles. Her hips twisted of their own accord in a sinuous, unceasing motion.

He sucked one nipple deep into his mouth, tugging on it gently, while flicking it with darting little jabs of his tongue. His hand went to her pubic mound and he groaned with satisfaction as he felt her heat and wetness.

With his hands still on her, he lifted his head from her breast. He gazed down at her, his eyes aglow. "I haven't said it for a while, Lindsay, and I truly don't expect you to say anything in return. But it's been bottled up inside for too long. I love you . . . more than I can say. I love you."

Her heart moved painfully in her chest. This time, she had to believe him. He'd had weeks to become certain of his feelings. Besides, his love was in his eyes, in the way he treated her, cared for her, cherished her— not just today, but every single moment they spent together.

It was her heart that answered him, not just her body. "I love you, too, Tim."

He inhaled sharply, then buried his face between her breasts. His hands went to her shoulders, clasping her as if he meant never to let her go.

She touched his hair and added, "I don't know if I *should* love you. There are still—"

He lifted his head and said fiercely, "No, don't! You can remind me of the problems tomorrow, if you must. Just say those words again, Lindsay—if you really mean it. Tell me you love me."

"I do mean it, Tim," she assured him. "I love you . . . very much."

He embraced her, holding her tightly against him. "I want to hear you say it while I'm inside you," he said hoarsely. "And I want to tell you, too. A thousand times. Over and over again."

He pulled away from her. The tremor in his fingers was visible as he reached toward the nightstand and took a foil-wrapped packet from the drawer. She had never seen him in the grip of such strong emotion; and her own emotions seemed to rise and swell in response until she was trembling with love and desire.

He paused, holding the rolled condom just above the tip of his erect penis. The words he spoke sounded as if they were ripped from him. "I don't want to use this."

He dropped the condom on the bed and turned to Lindsay. "I want to make you pregnant, Lindsay. I want you to have my child." He closed his eyes and she could see the tremor of desire vibrating in the muscles of his arms and chest. "God!"

His first words made Lindsay's womb contract. At the most fertile and sensual stage of her cycle, she felt intense need. She had to have Tim inside her—now. Filling her. And as he was, with no man-made barrier between them.

He turned his head away and picked up the condom from where he had dropped it. "I just wanted you to know." His voice was choked, thick with emotion.

Her hand snaked out. Her fingers wrapped around his wrist. "I want it, too. You don't need that, Tim. Not tonight." What was she saying? What was she doing? One tiny part of her was still rational enough to ask those questions, but her body was in charge now and it wanted Tim's seed within her. For an instant, she even seemed to feel herself big with child—Tim's child. Her breasts were swollen, exquisitely tender. She could feel the baby kicking.

The vision engulfed her in an unbearable surge of passion. She opened her knees wide, spreading herself in a delirium of desire, and reached for Tim. Her hand closed around his erection to guide him into her.

His eyes looked dazed. But he pulled away. "Lindsay, are you sure? It's really all right to do this?"

She knew what he meant. He was asking her if it was safe. But she didn't care. She *didn't want* it to be safe.

"Yes, yes," she whispered, impatiently. What was he waiting for? Couldn't he see how much she wanted him? How much she needed him . . . and what he could give her. He'd offered her the gift of life; did he mean to renege now?

No, he didn't. His face contorted with passion. "Oh, my God in heaven, Lindsay," he cried out as he plunged deep inside her.

Feeling him unshielded for the first time was so exquisite that Lindsay cried out, shuddered and climaxed almost at once.

But she wanted more.

Her hips lifted, drawing him in more deeply still, urging him to join her compelling rhythm.

"I love you," he told her, again and again.

"I love you," she echoed, as both of them spoke in a glorious counterpart to the steady pulse of their bodies' joining.

She was one with Tim, marching ever closer to fulfillment and release. A last, still-deeper thrust. His body convulsed and she felt his hot spill gush into her. The sensation threw her into a new paroxysm of pleasure. She was blind and deaf to everything except the power of the moment. As a low, undulating cry came from her lips, she felt the deepest part of herself opening, taking in the essence of himself that Tim had given her. Her legs twined tightly around his back, holding him inside until, some time later, she felt him begin to soften. Then, reluctantly, she released him.

He cradled her in his arms, murmuring how much he loved her.

Whispering the same words back to him, Lindsay began one by one to retrieve the pieces of her mind. When she had enough together that she could think again, one thought overrode all the others: What in the name of heaven had she done?

8

"YES? YOU'RE CERTAIN?" Lindsay held the phone tightly against her ear, as if the doctor's affirmation might leak out of her office and through the sturdy, soundproofed wall to Tim, next door. And then he would know what she had guessed since that night of her birthday some weeks ago: He was going to be a father.

She hung up the phone and stared straight ahead. Now it was definite. She'd have to tell Tim.

She'd had plenty of time to think about being pregnant and what it meant. She'd known she was from the first moment, though she'd tried to tell herself she might be wrong.

There'd been lots of confirmation, even before the doctor's call. Her body was changing; her breasts already felt fuller and tender, though, thank heaven, it wasn't yet time for her to experience any morning sickness.

Last week, the little marker on the home pregnancy test she'd bought and smuggled into the bathroom without Tim seeing it had turned pink. Definitely pink. She hadn't been able to kid herself that the test was wrong. After her doctor's call, it was official.

Even with all the time she'd had to get used to the idea, she still felt confused. Reason told her that this ought to be considered a tragedy. An unwed mother of forty. *Great!* Back to diapers and childhood illnesses and baby-sitter troubles. *Perfect!* And she'd be nearing sixty by the time this child was Dina's age.

Under her dismay was another emotion—a wild joy. Her love for Tim was going to bring forth life. And despite all the obvious wrongnesses of the situation, she couldn't help but feel that creation out of love was good and true and *right*.

However, being pregnant with Tim's baby might mean she'd lose him.

She'd gone over it again and again. He'd said he wanted to make her pregnant. But it was one thing in the heat of passion for a man to say he wished to impregnate his lover, another thing altogether for him to accept the responsibility for the next twenty years or so of that child's life.

He might even suggest she not have this baby— which would be the end, as far as Lindsay was concerned. Or his reaction might make it so evident that the baby was an unwanted burden that she would feel she had no other course but to set him free.

The possibilities were so daunting that for a ridiculous moment, she thought of not telling him ever.

But Tim had a right—a God-given ethical right—to know he had fathered a child.

She *had* to tell him. But by telling him, she might lose him. And the thought of being without Tim made a painful knot form in her chest—a knot that wasn't going to dissolve until she'd told him and found out what kind of future she was facing.

That being the case, she might as well get it over with. She dried her eyes, picked up the phone and punched the number that connected her to Nancy. "Is anybody with Tim right now?" she asked.

"No. Alice Waverly just left."

"Thanks, Nance," Lindsay said, then drew a deep breath and stood.

At Tim's door she lifted her hand to knock and saw that her knuckles were white. Her stomach churned—and it had nothing to do with the physical effects of pregnancy.

She rapped on the door too forcefully and when she heard Tim's "Come in," she thrust the door wide open, stepped inside, then closed the door behind her with a loud thud.

Tim was seated behind his desk, making notes on a legal pad. He looked up, grinning. "My, what an emphatic entrance!" His smile faded as he took in her facial expression. "Something wrong?"

"That sort of . . . depends," she said. Careful step by careful step, because her knees were shaking, she crossed the room and sat down in the easy chair.

Tim was frowning . . . waiting. . . .

She swallowed. When she spoke, her voice was brittle. "Well, you got your wish, Tim."

His expressive eyebrows lifted. She felt a new pang of dismay as she realized he had no idea what she was talking about. Would he even remember what he'd said at a moment fraught with passion?

She managed a choked laugh. "I'm pregnant. Isn't that something?"

Tim looked as if he'd turned to stone. His shoulders went rigid and there was no expression on his face.

"It's okay. Don't worry," she assured him. "I really don't expect you to—"

She stopped as, all at once, he broke free of his paralysis. He shoved his chair back and stood. Then he was rushing around the desk and collapsing onto his knees beside her chair. He wrapped his arms around her waist and buried his face in her lap, muttering choked sounds.

After a moment, she tentatively touched the back of his hair. At her touch, he lifted his head and stared deeply into her eyes.

To her astonishment, she saw that his rugged face was wet with tears. So, now she'd managed to make a strong man weep, she thought ironically. Was she supposed to comfort him? She could use some comforting herself.

And then she looked more closely at him, and wonder slowly bloomed in her mind. His tears were tears of joy.

"Oh, Lindsay, Lindsay," he said hoarsely. "I can't tell you how happy this makes me."

She couldn't speak. She had nothing to say, and tears filled her own eyes.

She held Tim's head closely against her, felt the strength of his arms embracing her waist and let the tears stream down her face. They kept running long after Tim had stood and drawn her up with him, his arms tight around her as if he meant their bodies to blend into one.

Finally she was able to speak again. "I was afraid . . . I thought . . . I didn't know . . ."

Tim chuckled and wiped her cheeks with the tip of one finger. "What are you trying to say, angel?"

Lindsay bent her head and rested her crown against his chest. "I honestly didn't know how you'd feel about this," she said in a small voice.

"Any questions about that, now?" She lifted her head to find him grinning, with one eyebrow lifted for ironic emphasis.

"No, I guess not. You don't seem to be exactly devastated." She swallowed, then managed a smile. "But, Tim, we've got to figure out what we're going to do about this."

He dropped his arms abruptly to his sides and took a step backward, away from her. "*Do* about it?" His frown was fierce. "Lindsay, you *are* planning to have this baby, aren't you? You're not considering—"

She stepped forward and touched his lips with her fingertips. "Hush! No, I'm *not* considering. I *want* to have this child—though, heaven knows, there are a million reasons why I shouldn't."

She had planned to assure him that she would never hold him to his responsibility for this child, nor force him to be more of a father than he wanted to be. She was ready now to say exactly that. But before she could begin, Tim's arms were around her again and he was saying with an exultancy in his tone that made her heart melt, "In that case, there's nothing to consider. We'll get married right away. It's simple."

She pulled back against the restraining circle of his arms, but he wouldn't let her go. "No, Tim. Wait! It doesn't have to be that way. That's what I was just about to tell you—that I don't *expect* you to marry me. I can take responsibility for this child. The last thing I want is for you to feel you have to marry me because of it."

"Hey, Lindsay . . ." He tipped her chin up so she was forced to look directly into his eyes. "This is me, remember? The guy who's already proposed to you once and wanted to propose . . . oh, no more than a million other times. I *want* to marry you. More than anything." He frowned. "I thought—but maybe I was wrong—that giving our baby a home and two parents and a solid base of security to grow up in would be more important to you than any objections you might have had to our marrying."

Silly objections, in Tim's opinion. She loved him. He knew that now, and not just because she'd said so. He knew she couldn't fake the feeling in her eyes when she looked at him. And now, with a baby on the way, she couldn't quibble over the age difference that seemed to bother her so much and him so little.

He tightened his grip on her. "Those things are more important. They've got to be. Tell me you agree, Lindsay."

"Yes," she replied, and when she heard her own voice speak the next two words, it was as if she were already hearing her response to the minister's most crucial question: "I do."

BUT THERE WERE THINGS that had to be accomplished before she and Tim could stand before the minister, and the most important of them had Lindsay driving up the coast to Santa Barbara two days later, on a Friday afternoon.

She had telephoned Dina the evening before and had told an awful lie, claiming that she had to be in Santa Barbara today to see a client, and could Dina have dinner with her before she drove back to L.A. She felt guilty about the falsehood, but if she had told her daughter the truth—that the reason for her visit was to talk about something important—Dina would have worried.

But from here on out, she intended to be completely candid, including telling Dina about her pregnancy. There would be no evasions, no "Surprise, honey!"s, a month or two down the line.

IN OTHER CIRCUMSTANCES, Lindsay would have enjoyed the campus. It had a pleasantly untidy, rural ambience, with eucalyptus trees waving their leaves in the breeze that came off the ocean.

She parked in the lot nearest Dina's dorm and found her daughter waiting on the front steps of the two-story building with the red tile roof.

Dina jumped up and came to meet her. "This is great," she said enthusiastically. "I didn't know you had any clients in Santa Barbara."

Lindsay closed her eyes for a moment. *No more lying!* "I don't, actually. I drove up because I need to talk to you."

Dina peered at her with a mixture of curiosity and alarm.

Lindsay suggested, "Let's take a stroll over to the lagoon, okay? There's something I have to tell you."

As soon as they were truly alone, she drew a deep breath and began. As candidly and succinctly as possible, she told Dina she was pregnant and that she and Tim had decided to get married almost at once.

Before she had quite finished, Dina gave a curt shake of her head, and said matter-of-factly, "I'm not sure I can deal with this."

Lindsay closed her eyes for a moment, searching herself for strength, then looked fully at her daughter and said in her gentlest voice, "I'm sorry, honey. I'm afraid you're going to have to deal with it. It's not going to go away." She put her hand on Dina's shoulder. "Please tell me what you're thinking."

Lindsay winced as Dina carefully stepped away from under her hand. Staring intently at the lagoon, she responded, "I can see you having an affair with Tim. But marrying him? And because you're pregnant?" She turned an anguished face toward Lindsay. "What would you say if it was me in this fix instead of you?"

"It's *not* a 'fix,'" Lindsay retorted. Hearing the edge in her voice, she inhaled deeply. It wouldn't help if she got angry with Dina. She had raised her daughter to be honest, and now she had to take the consequences.

But how to explain that *fix* was the wrong word? That Lindsay's situation was totally different from that of a teenage girl getting pregnant and *having* to marry the boy who'd gotten her that way?

Oh, yeah! Just how is it so different? You weren't considering marrying Tim before, were you? You'd pretty much decided it was out of the question, because of the age difference.

"Tim and I love each other. The baby... Well, that was an accident, I have to admit," she said in a determinedly mild tone.

Dina shook her head. "You should have listened to the lectures you gave me about birth control a couple of years ago. You made some pretty good points."

Anger again rose up in her, but she controlled it. "Okay, you've made *your* point. But it's too late for that now. What I'd like to know, if you can tell me, is which part of it bothers you so much. The marriage? It must have occurred to you that I might marry again. You even asked me if I thought Tim and I might get married someday. Remember?"

"I asked you and you said no," Dina retorted. "And that's exactly what I wanted you to say." She grimaced. "I shouldn't have said that. And I know I shouldn't feel that way. I ought to want you to be happy and have somebody. And part of me *does* want that. But not like this! And not a baby! I never thought you'd have a baby!"

Lindsay gazed at her sadly. There was the biggie, no matter what else Dina might say. She couldn't even blame her for feeling that way. Dina had been an only child for nineteen years—the sole focus of Lindsay's maternal love. And now, that was going to be changed. And Dina had had no say about it.

THEY CONTINUED TO TALK all during dinner. No matter what Lindsay said, she couldn't get past Dina's objections. When they returned to campus, Lindsay pulled the car up in front of Dina's dorm. At once, Dina's hand went to the door handle.

"Wait a sec," Lindsay said. "About the wedding. I haven't asked you if you'll come and I won't ask, because I don't want you to have to give me an answer tonight. But the ceremony's a week from tomorrow, at two o'clock in the afternoon, in the backyard at our house."

They had scheduled the wedding for the first weekend after the end of tax season. Tim's parents and three of his brothers and sisters and their families were flying out for the event. Tim would have family around him. Would she?

She had tried to reach her parents to tell them, but so far, she'd had no luck. They were off traveling somewhere in their unscheduled fashion. And she had an awful fear that Dina wouldn't be there, either.

She looked searchingly into her daughter's face. "It would mean—" her voice broke and she had to swallow before she could go on "—a great deal to me if you were there."

"I'll think about it," Dina promised, but her face was closed. She got out of the car and slammed the door.

LINDSAY STOOD in the bathroom, doubled over and trying to retch quietly so the eleven people downstairs in the living room waiting for her to join them for the night-before-the-wedding dinner wouldn't hear her.

The bride has morning sickness, Lindsay thought, dismayed. How charming! And it wasn't even morning. But she hadn't had a single bout of nausea until now, and this didn't feel exactly like the sickness she'd experienced while carrying Dina.

It must not be morning sickness, but sheer nerves.

And not because of those people downstairs, who, from the sounds of laughter and conversation that drifted upward, were having a perfectly jolly time. Two of them were her parents, whom she'd finally located in Texas and who had flown in for the wedding. After meeting Tim, they had pulled Lindsay aside to tell her how pleased they were that he would soon be their son-in-law.

The only comment that had made Lindsay flinch—a little—was when her mother offered hesitantly, "My! Tim certainly does look young for his age."

"No, Mother," Lindsay had said firmly. "He doesn't. He's twenty-nine. Almost thirty," she'd added hastily, as if that made all the difference.

All her mother had said was "Oh," and Lindsay decided it was paranoia that had made her hear disapproval in the monosyllable—especially when her father had boomed in, "Well, he seems like a fine man. Much nicer than that jerk, Martin."

"Why, Daddy," Lindsay had said, astonished. "You never *said* you thought Martin was a jerk."

"Well, he was . . . is," her father replied firmly. "And Tim's not."

It had gone just as well with the Reynolds clan. None of them had seemed in the slightest dismayed at meeting Lindsay, even though they must have recognized that the bride had a few years on the groom. The Reynoldses were so family-oriented that they were delighted that *their* Tim was to begin a family of his own.

Lindsay's parents and the whole Reynolds clan seemed to be getting along swimmingly, so there was absolutely no reason for her stomach to be churning over the prospect of the evening ahead.

No. It went much deeper than that. She hadn't heard a word from Dina; still had no idea if she would be here for the wedding tomorrow or not.

But there was more—dire thoughts that . . .

She heard footsteps on the stairs, then Tim's voice from outside the bathroom.

"Lindsay? Are you okay?"

"No," she answered bluntly, then bent over the toilet as her insides cramped again.

When she emerged, feeling raw inside but no longer ill, he was outside waiting for her. He put his arms around her and nuzzled her hair. "What a time for your first bout of morning sickness," he said sympathetically.

"I don't think that's what it was."

Tim drew back so he could examined her face. "You mean you might be sick—flu or something? We'll skip dinner and get you to a doctor."

Lindsay had to smile. He was showing such a touchingly exaggerated concern for her well-being these days, it was all she could do to convince him she was capable of carrying her own briefcase. "No, I don't need a doctor," she told him. In fact, the obstetrician, Dr. Mercador, had proclaimed her in excellent physical condition when he'd examined her last week, though he'd warned her that because of her age, she might not have as easy a time with this pregnancy as she'd had with Dina, twenty years ago.

She looked up at Tim and said what she'd been thinking and what was at the very root of her nausea a few moments before. "Tim, are you sure we're not making a mistake by getting married?"

Tim felt his insides clutch with a mixture of hurt and anger. Just when he thought happiness was in his grasp, her old doubts and fears had to emerge to get in the way. Snapping at her wouldn't help, though. He counted silently to five, then answered, "I'm sure *I'm* not making a mistake. Why do you think you might be, Lindsay? Not sure how you feel about me?"

"It's not that," she said quickly. "I do love you, Tim. You must know I do."

"I do know." He brushed her lips tenderly with his own. "But I just don't see anything else that could be bothering you. It's too late—wouldn't you say?—to worry about our relationship fouling up our business partnership. We're past that point. And anyway, we've been working together just fine for the last couple of months. I don't see any reason why it shouldn't go on working just as well—though, of course, we may have to make some adjustments when the baby comes." Suddenly he frowned. "Oh, honey! I'm sorry! I wasn't thinking. I know it's hard for you that Dina hasn't called or let you know if she'll be at the wedding. I'm a clod for forgetting."

"It bothers me that she hasn't called," she admitted. "But that's not all of it." She gripped his shoulders tightly with her hands. "It's you I'm thinking about,

Tim, and the age difference. It's no problem now, I guess. But what about—"

She stopped abruptly as a jovial male voice shouted from downstairs, "Hey, you two! If you're carrying on up there, then take a break! You've got the rest of your lives for that, and there are people starving down here."

Lindsay bit her lip, then called, "Coming, Dad."

Tim held her for a moment, then let her go. "We'll talk about it later."

LATE THAT NIGHT, Tim embraced his bride-to-be. Lindsay smiled as she fitted her body to his. The evening had been a happy one, and the warmth and good wishes of her family and his had succeeded in driving away her fears—or at least in covering them with other thoughts.

"Hey," she said lightly, "we're going to end up violating the old rule, you know. If we sleep together tonight, you'll hardly be able to avoid seeing me before the wedding tomorrow."

"I'll keep my hand over my eyes all morning," Tim promised. "Even if it means bumping into the furniture. What I'm *not* going to do is sleep alone. I've got you now, lady, and I'm not letting you go. Not even for one night."

He buried his face in her throat and Lindsay felt the familiar, welcome heat begin to build in her body.

And as Tim felt her flowing into him and her intoxicating scent fogging his brain with desire, he thought: *There was something we were supposed to talk about tonight.*

It mustn't be very important, though, or he'd remember what it was.

LINDSAY PEEKED anxiously down at the backyard from her bedroom window. The assembled guests were seated on rented folding chairs set up on the lawn. Her mother and Joanne were sitting together, chatting while they waited for the ceremony to begin.

Behind and beside the pair were the Reynolds clan and other friends and people from the office. Everyone she wanted to be here was here—except the single most important person in her life, apart from Tim.

And then she saw a slight, youthful figure slip into view from the side of the house where a gate led in from the street. Dina!

A smile so wide it hurt her face pulled back the corners of Lindsay's mouth. At that very moment, there was a tap on her door. Her father's voice called, "It's time, sugar. You ready?"

She flew to the door and opened it. "I sure am!"

A FEW WEEKS after the wedding, Lindsay tried in vain to button the skirt of her beige suit. Not even two-and-a-half months along, and the bulge of her belly was already quite pronounced. She hadn't intended to go into maternity clothes quite yet, but obviously it was time. She'd have to remember to ask the doctor when she saw him next week why she was getting so big so fast. She didn't think she was overeating.

She slipped the skirt down her legs, then hung it in the back of her closet, mentally bidding it and the rest of her normal wardrobe au revoir. She took out a dress she'd bought the week before—a sleeveless blue Empire-style maternity dress—and slipped it over her head.

Her breasts were noticeably larger now, and so tender that the mere touch of the dress's thin fabric sliding against her bra made her nipples pucker into tight little buds. And she was almost embarrassed to admit that she'd never felt so sexy in her life. All those hormones flooding her system had thrown her ripening body into a perpetual state of awareness. A mere glance from Tim, or just the thought of him, made her feel hot.

Thirty minutes later, she walked into her husband's office. He'd had an early-morning audit, and had left the house before her, so for him, this was her debut in maternity clothes. She closed the door behind her and pivoted for him to see. "Well, it's sacks from here on out," she said gaily.

Tim sprang to his feet and came toward her, but stopped a few feet short. He expelled a sharp breath. "Lindsay! You look absolutely gorgeous." He meant it. Her face was fuller, softer. And he'd studied her breasts, concealed now by the first maternity dress he'd seen her in, enough to have a vivid mental picture of them—lush, full, with a tracery of blue veins beginning to appear beneath the skin.

The thought that he was responsible for these magnificent changes in her, that he and she together had created the life now swelling within her, caused a rush of desire in Tim. He could feel himself hardening, just from looking at her.

She had assured him that she wasn't breakable, when he'd been inclined to treat her with too much gentleness. And she'd told him candidly that her desire for him seemed, if anything, to be increased by pregnancy.

His gaze slid down her body, lingering adoringly on every inch of her. And then he lifted his eyes. There was a faint flush on her face. And lower, he saw two points where her nipples poked against the blue cloth. She wanted him; and if it was half as badly as he wanted her, it was plenty.

He said, "Lindsay, lock the door."

A frown flickered between her narrow brows. "The door?"

He returned to his desk and picked up the phone. "Nancy, hold our calls, okay? We're going to be in conference for a while."

Lindsay gasped, then laughed, all in one breath. As he put down the receiver, she remarked, "You wicked, wicked man."

"One of the advantages of working together."

She crossed the room, snapped the dead bolt in place, then turned back to look around the office. "But where?"

He took the seat and back cushions from the easy chairs and dropped them on the floor, then carefully lined them up to make an impromptu bed. "There," he told her.

She made as if to sit down on the cushions. But Tim stopped her. "Wait, Lindsay. I want to undress you."

That was one of the things she loved about him, she thought—that he never seemed to tire of the small sensual attentions that meant so much. How many times had he undressed her now? And still he acted as if it were the first time he had reverently uncovered her for his eyes' and hands' delight.

He unzipped the smocklike dress and lifted it over her head, then unhooked her maternity bra and slipped it off her shoulders. His gaze fixed on her breasts with their darkened nipples and he let out a groan as he gently covered one with his hand. "So lovely," he breathed.

Feeling intense pleasure at his license to touch, to love, to care, Tim smoothed his hand over the protruding curve of Lindsay's belly. All that covered her now were thin panties. She'd told him it would be a few weeks yet before she would feel the baby move. He could hardly wait. The thought of actually putting his hand where it rested now and feeling his child kicking made a breathtaking tide of emotion surge up within him.

Lindsay looked down at Tim's hand on her swollen abdomen and frowned. "I'm getting so big so fast," she observed. "I don't think I was showing nearly so soon with Dina." She let out a light laugh. "Or maybe I'm just not remembering properly. It's been an awfully long time."

Then she looked at Tim. "And you have far too many clothes on. I feel at a decided disadvantage here."

Tim smiled. "We can't have that." He spread his arms wide. "Work your will on me, woman." He winked. "Mind you, I'm only letting you have your way with me because you're pregnant, and pregnant women have to be humored."

She began to undo the buttons on his shirt. "I expect you to remember that, sir! Especially when I start craving sauerkraut in the middle of the night."

He sighed with pleasure as she spread open the sides of his shirt and smoothed her palms down the firm muscles of his chest. "Have you had any cravings yet?" he asked, curious.

She smiled. He was endlessly interested in the details of her pregnancy. "Not yet." She lowered her voice to a sultry murmur. "Not for food, anyway."

His eyes twinkled. "Oh?" he responded blandly. "What other kinds of cravings could there be?"

"You know!"

"Then I'd better do my best to satisfy them."

"You do, Tim. Believe me, you do!" she said fervently. She could see by the bulge beneath his trousers that he was already fully aroused. Not that there was anything unusual about that; he seemed always ready to make love to her. She had decided some time back that Tim was just naturally highly sexed. Which was just fine with her, since she was the grateful recipient. But now, for some reason, she remembered Nancy's remark about the advantages of a man close to his sexual prime. Tim's readiness for lovemaking must be partially a result of his youth.

It was an uncomfortable thought and she pushed it determinedly aside. At some point, she'd made a decision not to think about that ten-year age gap. They were married now, for better or for worse—and so far, it was *better* all the way.

She undid his belt, then unbuttoned and unzipped his trousers. As he stepped out of them, she was already peeling his shorts down his legs. As she leaned over, the tip of his erection brushed her cheek. Very convenient, she reflected.

Leaving Tim to dispose of his underwear without her help, she knelt and took him in her mouth. She never tired of tasting and touching him there, where he was smooth as silk and hard as iron. And Tim seemed not to have tired of it, either, for he let out a low growl of satisfaction.

Then he sank down beside her on the cushions and kissed her, using his tongue to explore, tease, tantalize.

Deliberately Lindsay brushed her ultrasensitive nipples lightly back and forth against his chest. The friction against his chest hair soon had her taut and trembling with need and, as she continued the side-to-side motion, she stroked his thighs, then his buttocks, then moved again to his front to hold his hard, hot length in her hand.

Tim pulled her down on their improvised bed and wrapped his arms around her, then buried his face in the curve of her throat. His lips opened to nibble and taste, and he moved one hand to gently cover her breast. Delicately, obviously conscious of how sensitive she was right now, he teased her nipple with his fingertips. Lindsay's back arched as a shaft of heat struck directly at her inner core.

He bent his head. His lips closed gently over her tight, hard nipple. His eyes open, to be alert to the slightest hint that he might be causing pain, he stroked her with his tongue. Its motion, hot and wet, inflamed her. She felt as if her breasts were swelling visibly. Low down, her body opened, pulsing with the need for Tim to fill her.

He slid lower on the cushions, his mouth making a leisurely exploration of her expanding body. She felt as if his tongue left not one square inch of her untouched. And everywhere he kissed, her body burned, adding to the heat gathering between her thighs.

As he moved lower, tantalizingly lower, she tightened with anticipation. Finally his mouth was searing through her passion-soaked panties. It was the first she'd realized in quite some time that she was still wearing anything at all.

He rolled the flimsy garment off her hips, down her legs, caressing as he went. Then, as she opened her legs to him in invitation, he nibbled his way back up from her ankles. It was an effort for her to hold still as he buried his face between her legs.

She flickered her eyelids open. She could see Tim's head, and above that the swell of her belly, then her full, taut breasts.

She felt ripe, round, and so highly charged sexually that it was no surprise when Tim's mouth quickly brought her to a sweet release.

And then, when she was certain he would lever himself over her and enter her, he *did* surprise her, by pulling her up to a sitting position. He reversed things so that he was lying on his back and she, straddling his hips. She gladly took his cue and lifted, then lowered herself onto him—slowly, to savor every millimeter of his length sliding into her.

Their fit was beyond perfection. She was tight around him, almost to the point of her feeling that he was an actual part of her. As she slipped up and down around him, she could feel a volcano building inside her, getting ready to erupt.

He reached up and delicately fingered her nipples. Her mouth opened as a cry forced its way up her throat. She remembered where they were and stifled the sound by clamping her lips together.

Tim's face was rapt with passion, his pupils dark. But he blinked once and said, "Don't worry about making noise. Soundproofing, remember?"

She did remember—though it hadn't been with anything of this sort in mind that they'd soundproofed both their offices. Relieved, she let the cry well up as she pressed down hard on Tim, taking his full length. His hips jerked and his hoarse shout of triumph and relief mingled with her own sounds as the volcano exploded, rippling such intense waves of pleasure through her that she was flung limp onto Tim's chest.

A few moments later, within the circle of his arms, she murmured, "I hope you don't mind that I'm so insatiable these days. Well . . . even *more* insatiable," she corrected herself. "I guess I was pretty voracious before I got pregnant."

Tim's eyebrows mimed amused astonishment. "Wrong words, Lindsay. Just an incredibly sexy woman. Every man's dream. And you're mine, all mine," he said with exaggerated glee, then added more soberly, "I'm sure glad you're not one of those women who don't enjoy sex while they're pregnant." He'd been reading up on pregnancy and its effects so he'd have some inkling of what to expect.

The cushions had slipped and Lindsay's bare hip was on the carpet. But she didn't mind. She'd never felt so contented, so replete. "It helps that I haven't had morning sickness," she explained. Apparently she'd been right, and her bout the night before the wedding had been due solely to nerves. "I can imagine it wouldn't be much fun making love if you were nauseated all the time."

Tim grimaced. "Sounds awful. I guess we should count our blessings."

"Tim," Lindsay said, "you know we may not be able to make love the last few weeks before the baby comes."

"Of course, I know that!" he said indignantly.

She snuggled closer. "But we'll be able to do...other things." She smiled.

9

As LINDSAY HUNG UP her office phone, Dr. Mercador's words ricocheted around in her head. She sat for a moment until the news stopped bouncing off her mental walls and she was able to think coherently.

She couldn't tell Tim now. He had one of their most important clients coming in this afternoon. And news like what she had to impart would put any man off his stride.

Tonight at dinner, she decided.

No. *After* dinner. She'd been taking walks for exercise, often after their evening meal, now that it stayed light so long. Tim usually went with her. She could tell him then, though maybe it would be better if he was sitting down....

It WAS the soft gray time of day, after the sun had set. In silence, they walked leisurely to a nearby park.

Lindsay paused near a picnic table that stood beneath an oak tree. The perfect spot, she thought dryly. If Tim passed out from shock, he'd have something to lie on besides the grass.

Tim's fingers were laced in hers. "Feeling tired?" he asked sympathetically.

"I would like to sit for a minute."

She maneuvered herself onto the attached bench, careful not to bump her belly against the edge of the table. Tim sat down opposite her. "Something wrong, Lindsay? You've been pretty quiet."

She drew a deep breath. "Dr. Mercador called this afternoon, with the results of my tests." Seeing the alarm on his face, she leaned across the table to squeeze his hand reassuringly. "It's okay," she said quickly. "The babies are perfectly healthy."

"Thank heaven! I was afraid for a minute that—" He broke off and did a classic double take, "Did I hear you right, Lindsay? I thought you said—"

"Babies," she confirmed with a nod. "It's twins. A boy and a girl."

Tim had jumped up and came around to her side of the table so he could put his arm around her.

"That's great news. Incredible, fantastic news!"

"You may not think so when, between the two of them, there's a baby crying all night long."

"Yes, I know it'll make things tough at times, but . . . wow!"

"You said that before." His excitement was so infectious that some of Lindsay's shock dissipated. Maybe it was a good thing, after all. At first, she had seen only the difficulties.

He picked up her hand from where it rested on the tabletop and pressed a kiss to her fingertips. "You know, Lindsay, I wouldn't have said anything before, but I've always wanted to have more than one kid."

Lindsay felt a pang as the implication of his words sank in: the part he hadn't said—that the only way he could have more than one child with her was via a multiple birth—and its corollary—that if he'd married a younger woman, one not already past her best child-bearing years, he wouldn't have needed to have twins to complete his family.

Was she cheating him? Would he look back with regret? She shivered at the idea.

Tim gazed at her, concerned. "Are you feeling chilly, love? Maybe we'd better get back."

"No, I'm fine," she said, trying to console herself with the thought that at least she was giving Tim *two* children. She hoped that was enough.

She smiled her biggest, brightest smile. "Well, I guess we'd better start thinking of names for twins. I don't know about you, but I'm decidedly against names that begin with the same initial."

"I agree. And nothing that rhymes, either."

"Oh, definitely. We want them to be individuals."

He grinned "Course, with a boy and a girl, that won't be that big a problem." He paused for a long moment. "Uh, Lindsay, I just thought of something. Twins run in families, right?"

"So I've always heard. But I'm sure none of my relatives has ever had twins. Tim . . . ?"

He nodded, putting on a furtive expression.

She mimed a horrified glare. "So it's all *your* fault."

"Guilty as charged." He looped both arms around her and hugged her, then smoothed one hand down over her abdomen. She knew he loved to touch her there and that he was waiting, as she was, for the joyous moment when she would first feel the movement of the child—children.

"Nothing yet?" he asked.

"It's still early."

"I know." But he left his hand on her stomach. He winked. "Checking it out is a great excuse to touch you, though."

"Since when," she demanded lovingly, "have you ever needed an excuse?"

Under the table, she put her hand on his knee, then drew her palm slowly up his thigh. Her fingertips brushed his crotch. "Oh, dear," she said, pretending to be dismayed. "I *am* chilly, after all. Don't you think we'd better hurry home?"

"WELL, you're certainly blooming," remarked Joanne.

Lindsay had to smile. "More than you know." The two women had met at their favorite patio restaurant. Now, in early July, the work was fairly light for Lindsay at the office and she'd felt she could take a nice long lunch to visit with Joanne. She leaned forward and said conspiratorially, "It's twins."

"No!" Joanne shook her head. "When you do something, Lindsay Ames . . . uh, Reynolds, you do it with a vengeance. How does Tim feel about it?"

"Overjoyed," Lindsay said, trying not to think about the uncomfortable thoughts she'd had the night before.

"Well, that's good. What about Dina? Have you told her?"

Lindsay nodded slowly. Dina was the only cloud on her horizon. Her daughter had only visited home twice since the wedding. On those visits, she had been perfectly polite—but distant. The easy warmth between them was gone. And Lindsay couldn't help but notice that Dina never let her eyes drift to her mother's growing belly.

A few weeks ago, Dina had called to announce that she'd decided to attend summer school and wouldn't be home until August. Last night, when Lindsay had told Dina on the phone that she was to have both a baby brother and a sister, Lindsay had been totally unable to gauge her reaction from her polite congratulations.

"And?" Joanne prompted.

"I don't know," Lindsay admitted with a sigh. "But she said she was coming home tomorrow for the weekend, so I ought to be able to get more of a sense of how she feels about it then—I hope." She gave Joanne a tight smile. "On to more pleasant topics. Tim sold his condo, and he even got his asking price."

LINDSAY AND TIM were just finishing up a late and leisurely Saturday breakfast the next morning when they heard a car pull up in the driveway.

"Dina?" Tim asked.

Lindsay nodded.

"Should I vanish now or later?"

"Maybe later, if you don't mind," Lindsay said. "But there's no need for you to go dashing off right away."

"Okay. I'll try to time it so it's not too obvious."

"Your timing is always impeccable," she murmured, then, hearing the front door open and close, she called, "We're in the kitchen, hon."

Dina came into the room a moment later, dressed in shorts and a tank top. "Hi, Mom. Hi, Tim. How are you?"

"Fine," Lindsay said automatically. "Want some coffee? There's a little left and I can make another pot."

Dina shrugged. "Sure. I guess."

Lindsay pushed back her chair and rose carefully, as she had to do everything these days, with the developing bulk of the babies throwing off her sense of balance.

Dina's eyes widened. "You're so big!" There was accusation, even disgust in her tone.

Lindsay gritted her teeth, but forced her voice to remain light. "It happens that way when you get two for the price of one."

She went to the counter and poured Dina the last of the coffee, then started another pot. By the time she was done, Tim had gotten Dina talking about school and the courses she was taking this summer. Dina had developed an interest in anthropology and was thinking of making it her major in the fall.

But Dina had something on her mind; Lindsay's motherly radar picked up on the girl's hesitation and the way Dina's eyes never once met hers directly.

She stifled an internal sigh. She hoped it wasn't going to be *too* unpleasant; but even an unpleasant conversation would be better than the noncommunication they'd been having lately.

Tim caught Lindsay's eye and rose. "Well, I've got a bunch of errands to run. Anything you need, Lindsay, that isn't on the list?"

"No, thanks, Tim," she replied.

He leaned over to kiss her cheek and said goodbye to Dina.

Dina sat stiffly, her hands clasped on the table in front of her. Lindsay looked at her, waiting.

Dina drew a deep breath. "There's something I have to tell you, Mom. And I don't think you're going to like it."

Lindsay tensed, but forced herself not to show it. "Try me," she prompted encouragingly.

"This summer, after summer school gets out—" Dina paused, then said all in a rush "—I'm going to spend the rest of my vacation in New York with Dad."

"With Dad?" Lindsay couldn't keep the astonishment out of her voice.

Dina nodded. "We've been talking on the phone some, lately. You and Tim and your being pregnant and all—well, I guess it made me realize I have two parents. I'd had you to myself for so long, but now I don't, and I really didn't know Dad at all. Not since I was just a kid. So I called him a few times."

Lindsay understood, and though she was sorry that Dina felt so alienated from her now, she was relieved that her alienation had brought about a rapprochement with Martin.

Dina went on before Lindsay could say anything. "And from a couple of things that Dad said, I realized that he regretted that we hadn't seen more of each other. So I called him a few days ago and asked if I could come stay with him in August, and he said I could. He's paying my plane fare, too. I knew you wouldn't want to."

"You knew wrong, Dina," Lindsay said forcefully. "I'd have been glad to pay your air fare. And I think it's great that you and Dad are going to spend some time together."

Dina stared at her, then blinked as moisture formed in her eyes. "You do, Mom? I thought . . ." The tears flowed and Lindsay got up, carefully, to give her daughter a hug.

"I FEEL LIKE A BELLY with feet," Lindsay grumbled as she observed her reflection in the bedroom-dresser mirror. She could see none of the fabled "glow of pregnancy." Her face was pinched and drawn, and there were dark circles beneath her eyes. She stepped back from the mirror to check the pink dress she had just put on for the Jensens' Labor Day party. All she could see was the bulge in front of her, draped by the folds of her dress.

She looked down past the hem of her dress. Her legs and ankles were still slim, but she had to wear flat-heeled shoes for safety's sake. "What a frump," she commented irritably.

Tim came out of the bathroom, pulling the knot of his tie into place. "What'd you say, angel? I didn't—"

He broke off as his gaze fastened on his wife. Her dress was a soft, creamy pink, and it swooped low in front to reveal her cleavage, the fabric clinging to the full undercurve of her breasts. The arc of her belly was a shape that pleased his eye immensely. She looked ripe and beautiful—the essence of womanhood.

Although he'd noticed the shadows under her eyes and worried that she wasn't getting enough sleep, the mauve smudges did not detract one bit from her loveliness. If anything, they gave her a look of vulnerability that made his heart ache with love.

"You look wonderful, Lindsay," he breathed.

"Don't be kind to me, Tim," she said peevishly. "I know exactly how I look."

He shook his head uncomprehendingly. Pregnant women were supposed to be moody; and lately, Lindsay had proved the assertion to be true, snapping at him once or twice, just like now. He resolved to be patient and ignore her flare-ups, because over the past few months his love for her had grown. Watching her body swell with their children was a profound experience for him and he cherished the changes in her body that he observed taking place day by day. He never tired of looking at her, never tired of touching her belly to feel the movements of the twins.

And touching her for that reason often led to touching her for other reasons. Lately, her bulkiness had meant they'd had to become more inventive when making love.

She'd turned back to face the mirror and scowled at her reflection. Was it possible that she really couldn't see how lovely she looked?

"You may not believe me, Lindsay, but you'll be the most beautiful woman at the party tonight."

Lindsay refused to be soothed. She hadn't felt well all day today. Indigestion, probably; but it made her feel unusually cranky.

Cranky. Ugly. Poor Tim, she thought, saddled with such a wife. "I'm sorry, Tim. I'm just having a bad da-a-ay. . . ." The last word ended on a wail as, without warning, she burst into tears.

He held her for a while, then carefully blotted her eyes and cheeks with his handkerchief. He hid a smile. She was just being . . . pregnant.

MINDFUL OF HER MOOD, Tim stuck close to Lindsay's side for the first hour of the Jensons' party. He also commandeered a chair for her, so she wouldn't have to be on her feet.

Lindsay's mood gradually improved; she felt a little like a queen receiving her courtiers, as many of the Jensons' guests stopped to say hello and chat with her and Tim.

But then, portly, merry Roland Jenson pried Tim away, insisting on showing him his newly converted basement poolroom. Lindsay stayed where she was.

When Tim returned to the room, he met her eye, smiled, then started toward her, but was stopped part-way by another client of theirs, a friend of Roland Jenson's. Tim glanced at Lindsay and she signaled that she was doing just fine on her own. She was a big girl—very big, she thought ruefully, staring down at her bulging lap. She didn't have to have her husband constantly dancing attendance.

A moment later, she regretted not having waved Tim over to her. A woman joined the group he was in—a slim young blonde in a low-cut white dress that was tight enough to show that she had absolutely no stomach at all.

Lindsay was too far away to hear what was being said, but she could see the blonde animatedly addressing Tim. Lindsay knew she had no reason to feel jealous, but all the same she did. The woman was obviously interested in Tim.

She had too much pride to go over and insinuate herself into the group. But she also didn't have to sit here and watch.

The pang of jealousy felt like a hollowness in her stomach. No wonder! She hadn't eaten much all day because of that indigestion.

As usual, the Jensons had put on a lavish buffet. She got up and waddled toward the buffet.

Only one person was already there—a man filling his plate. He had his back to her as she approached, but when she got near the edge of the table, he turned and gave her a polite, purely social smile.

It was Adam Holloway, the man she'd met last January. His eyes widened. "Is it . . . Lindsay?"

"Yes. Hello, Adam." A mere three-quarters of a year ago, he'd been interested enough in her to ask her out. And now, he'd barely recognized her. "How are you?"

"Fine. Just fine," he said, then glanced again at her belly. "No need to ask how you are. I can see."

"Pregnant," she added unnecessarily. The strange, unpleasant sensations she'd felt all day were back. A sharp pain ripped through her, and she gasped.

Adam looked more closely at her. "*Are* you all right, Lindsay?"

"No. No, I'm not." She grabbed the edge of the table for support. "Get my husband, will you please, Adam? He's right over there."

GRIM-FACED, Tim walked back and forth in the hospital waiting room. The doctor had told him that Lindsay's pain had been the onset of labor—three months early! If they couldn't stop it, the twins would be so premature that they'd have at best only a fifty-fifty chance of survival.

As Tim paced to one end of the room, a man seated in a nearby easy chair looked up at him with a quizzical expression. "Your first?"

"Yes," Tim replied tersely, unwilling to explain that whatever they were doing to Lindsay, it was not a normal birth.

"I thought so. Relax, guy. It won't help if you wear yourself out. Take it from me. I've—"

"Tim?"

Tim turned to see Dina standing in the doorway of the waiting room. School had started at U.C.S.B. and he had called her at her dorm shortly after they'd wheeled Lindsay away, over two hours ago. She must have started driving the moment she'd hung up the phone.

He hurried over to her and gave her a big hug.

"How's Mom?" she asked when he released her. "Is she going to be okay?"

"She'll be fine," Tim said with more confidence than he felt. The doctor had assured him that Lindsay herself was in no danger, but he couldn't quite rid himself of his fear. Speeding to the hospital, she'd been white-faced with pain. She'd hardly spoken, except to blurt out once, "Tim, I think I'm bleeding."

"It's the twins we have to worry about," he said, putting his arm around Dina and steering her toward a vacant couch.

Having Dina there made the waiting easier. Being with someone who cared about Lindsay almost as much as he did was infinitely preferable to anguished pacing alone. Even so, the minutes crawled. It was after four in the morning when a young man in doctor's whites came to the door of the waiting room. "Mr. Reynolds?"

Tim bounded forward with Dina close on his heels. The physician hastened to assure him, "We've stopped labor and your wife is stable. She's sleeping now, so you might as well go home and get some rest."

"The babies? Will they be all right?"

"They're all right at this point. Naturally, they'll have a much better chance if they can be brought to full term. Dr. Mercador will be talking to you and your wife about that. In the meantime, get some rest."

Tim nodded, then put his arm around Dina's shoulders. "Come on, kiddo. We might as well go home."

10

"YOU'RE GOING TO HAVE to stay in bed? For three months? That's awful," Dina said sympathetically.

Lying in the hospital bed, Lindsay smiled up at her daughter. "If that's what I've got to do, that's what I've got to do," she replied. Dr. Mercador had been very explicit in his instructions. "Flat on your back," he'd said. "I don't even want you getting up to go to the bathroom. You'll have to take sponge baths and learn to use a bedpan. Any violation of the rules and I'm putting you back in the hospital."

Lindsay wasn't about to argue—not when she knew that following the doctor's orders was absolutely necessary.

The one good thing to come out of this was that Dina was here; not only here, but talking naturally and easily to her mother for the first time since Lindsay had told her of her pregnancy.

Dina reached over and squeezed Lindsay's shoulder. "I'm sorry I've been such a drip, Mom. Last night— when Tim and I were waiting to hear?"

Lindsay nodded. She could imagine the agony the two of them had gone through. She had seen traces of it in Tim's face when she'd seen him earlier that morning.

"Well, I really wanted the twins to be okay." Dina swallowed, then went on in a rush, "Anyway, it's okay about you and Tim and the twins and . . . everything."

More than anything, Lindsay wanted to sit bolt upright and envelop her daughter in a huge hug. But she had to content herself with giving Dina's hand an extra-warm squeeze. "That's great, Dina. I'm really glad. And thanks."

Dina flushed, then prompted, "Do you want to hear how my visit with Dad went?"

"Love to," Lindsay told her. "I didn't ask before, because I figured if you wanted to tell me, you would."

Dina considered. "It was . . . good. Dad's got this girlfriend and she's okay, too. Very business-oriented, just like him." She giggled. "Two peas in a pod. They actually sit around discussing corporate mergers. Can you believe it?"

Knowing Martin, Lindsay could. And she found that she was glad for Martin that he'd found someone who, apparently, was right for him—just as she'd found Tim.

Dina continued thoughtfully: "But the main thing is, Dad and I did a lot of talking and I think we got to be friends. Not like I am with you, but . . . friends."

"That's great," Lindsay said. "I'm glad." And even gladder that Dina was thinking of her as a good friend again.

The door of the room opened, and Lindsay's heart lurched at the sight of Tim. When he'd been there briefly earlier, he'd kissed her, held her hand and expressed his love and relief. But before they'd had a chance to really discuss Dr. Mercador's orders for Lindsay's immediate future, Dina had come in. After a few minutes, Tim had announced that he had errands he needed to do, leaving Lindsay and Dina to talk.

The nature of at least one of his errands was apparent, for he was carrying an enormous bouquet of her favorite fall flowers—chrysanthemums in shades of russet and gold.

Now it was Dina's turn to be tactful. "Well, I guess I'd better get going. I need to head back to school." She leaned over to kiss Lindsay, then suggested, "If you want, I could come home next weekend. Since you're going to be laid up, Mom, Tim might need some help around the house."

"That's really nice of you, honey."

Tim said warmly to Dina, "I sure could use some help. We'll expect you next weekend, then."

When the door had closed behind Dina, Lindsay looked up adoringly at Tim. "The flowers are beautiful." Her voice was husky. "And you're pretty terrific yourself, fella."

"So are you, lady." Such a close brush with tragedy had brought home even more strongly what he already knew—what a treasure he had in Lindsay and the babies.

He placed his bouquet on the dresser. "No sense in scrounging up a vase for these when you're going home so soon." He returned to her bedside, picked up her hand and brought it to his lips.

A nurse stuck her head in the door. "Mrs. Reynolds? We need to get you dressed now. Doctor says you can go home any time."

LINDSAY SNUGGLED BACK against the pillows in the bedroom she and Tim shared. She could do this—stay in bed for the next three months. Not that she had a choice.

But it wouldn't be all that bad. She was allowed to elevate her head and shoulders enough to read and eat and watch TV. She'd find a way to make the time pass.

She was more worried about how Tim would cope. So far, though, he was coping extraordinarily well. Buying flowers wasn't all he'd done that morning during his absence from the hospital. He'd also borrowed a friend's station wagon and made a nest of blankets and pillows in the back so Lindsay could remain in a reclining position going home, thus avoiding the indignity of an ambulance. Then he'd carried her all the way upstairs.

And when he'd deposited her gently on their bed, she'd seen that somehow he'd also found the time to prepare the room. There were books and magazines within her reach on the nightstand, right next to the remote-control unit for the brand-new TV he'd hooked up at the foot of the bed.

He entered the room now, carrying lunch on a tray. She marveled, "I don't know how you did all this in such a short time."

He grinned. "I'm an accountant, I'm organized."

He put the tray on the side table, then adjusted the pillows behind Lindsay's back as she eased into a sitting position. "That's okay? You're not sitting up too far?" he asked anxiously as he handed her the tray.

"It's fine." Balancing the tray on her belly wasn't easy, she soon discovered. It tended to tilt.

Tim noticed the trouble she was having. "I'll get a bed table...and anything else you need. I know this is going to be tough on you, Lindsay. I want you to be as comfortable as possible."

"I can see that. And you're doing a great job." She swallowed the last of her soup. "But I'm more worried about you, Tim."

"Me? I'm not the one who has to lie in bed."

"No, but you're the one who'll have to take up the slack. Not only here, but at work." Lindsay gave a little shake of her head. "Maybe you'd better hire someone to fill in for me."

"Nonsense," Tim said assuringly. "It's not tax time, after all."

"But still, there's a lot to do," Lindsay insisted. An idea struck her. "I know. There're a lot of things—bookkeeping chores, for instance—that I could do right here, if you'd bring records home and—"

Tim cut her off. "Absolutely not. And besides, it isn't necessary, Lindsay. I'll be able to handle everything just fine."

LORD, SHE WAS LUCKY to have Tim, Lindsay thought the next evening at dinnertime. As promised, he had gotten her a bed table. It had an arm that swung over in front of her. She could put her food on it while she ate, prop books on it, all kinds of handy things.

He had also fixed a delicious dinner—fish, a salad, and crisp, green vegetables. Now he was down in the kitchen, washing up.

She was indeed lucky to have him; but how lucky was *he?* It wasn't fair for him to have to do everything, her nothing. She had voiced that thought during dinner and he had said, with astonishment in his voice, "But Lindsay, you're doing the most important job of all—giving our children the best possible chance at life."

She couldn't argue with Tim over that one, but still, she wished she didn't feel like such a burden on him. And it was only beginning. There were weeks and weeks of this ahead.

Tim came in, holding a plastic bottle of the pink lotion she'd been using. It wouldn't help her stretch marks—no miracle product could eliminate those—but as her skin stretched, it itched, and the lotion helped that a lot.

"We haven't done this for several days," he said, grinning. "Can't let ourselves get behind."

Lindsay had to smile in return. Before premature labor had sent her to the hospital, Tim had proclaimed himself responsible for the condition of her skin. His smoothing on of the lotion had become a highly erotic ritual. It couldn't be that now, of course—not after what Dr. Mercador had told her. Tim knew the rules; the doctor had talked to him, too. But there was no harm in letting him soothe her skin with his hands.

Moving with the exaggerated care with which she did everything these days, Lindsay pulled up her nightgown and lifted her shoulders so Tim could help her pull the garment off over her head. She lay back against the pillows.

He sat down on the edge of the bed and began, as he often did, by applying lotion to her hands and arms. She had told him it wasn't necessary, that her arms weren't the part of her that itched, but Tim insisted that if he was going to do a job, he meant to do it thoroughly. So he rubbed lotion into her palms and fingers, bending and massaging them, then moved up her arms, paying special attention to the sensitive places.

Nice.

Then he poured a small pool of lotion on the area she had once liked to think of as her midriff. Using that pool as a center, he smoothed lotion over the slope of her belly; with his other hand, he dabbed lotion on the underside of one breast.

Lindsay inhaled sharply as she felt his fingertips ascending her various curves. For some reason, she had thought that the trauma of nearly losing the twins would have damped her erotic response to Tim's touch.

Wrong, wrong, wrong! she realized as she felt a familiar heat pouring through her. "Tim . . ." Her voice emerged huskily, sounding more like an encouragement than the warning she had meant it to be.

He certainly took it as encouragement. Lightly teasing her nipple with one hand, he slid his other hand over the mound of her belly. His fingers probed delicately in her pubic hair.

Her hips tilted, offering him easier access, even as her mind shrieked "No!" and her hand clamped around his wrist. "Tim, stop it!" she snapped. "You know we can't do that!"

"What?" His brow furrowed.

"Dr. Mercador must have told you. No lovemaking."

"Well, sure. I wasn't planning to . . . er, climb on top of you or anything."

She shook her head. Damn doctors! She'd assumed he'd explained to Tim as thoroughly as he'd explained to her.

Her voice was small, apologetic. "I'm sorry, Tim. I thought you knew. I can't . . . climax. I mean, I'm not supposed to. Dr. Mercador said that in some cases, the internal contractions . . . *could* start labor."

Tim took his hands away from her, his face stunned-looking. "I didn't know." But then he smiled. "Okay. Let's finish putting the lotion on. I'll be very . . . discreet about it, I promise."

He was true to his word. Staying strictly on her belly where the skin was stretching the most, he applied the lotion in a businesslike manner. Lindsay watched sadly as he touched her. Their lovemaking was precious to her, but it would have to be foregone—at least *her* side of it would. Her dismay lightened slightly as she realized she wouldn't have to be deprived of everything. She could still please and satisfy Tim.

TIM FELT EMBARRASSED, but even more, he was angry at Dr. Mercador for not telling him everything he needed to know. He never would have touched Lindsay in that way if he'd dreamed—

His hands moved over her briskly, trying not to be seductive. Just a minute longer and he'd have the lotion all rubbed in.

He had both hands on her belly when he felt motion beneath his palm. Feeling the babies within her never ceased to stir his emotions. Now, when they'd been so recently in danger, the feeling of their life beneath his palms made such an intense emotion well up in him that he quickly averted his eyes. He couldn't look at Lindsay, for fear she might see in his face the echoes of the terrible fear that had gripped him during that long night of waiting.

He turned his head and studied the blank TV screen at the foot of the bed, fighting for control.

At that moment, Lindsay, who had been lost in thought, looked up at Tim. He was briskly making sure the last of the lotion had penetrated her skin, but his head was turned away from her.

A pain ripped through her, frightening her until she realized it was emotional pain she was feeling, not physical. He couldn't bear to look at her. Bulging as she was, she must have become an unpleasant sight in his eyes. Perhaps the way he'd touched her before had been only from a sense of duty.

She had to swallow twice to dislodge the jagged lump in her throat. Then she said briskly, brightly, "I think that's plenty, Tim. Thanks."

He stood near the edge of the bed, putting the top back on the lotion bottle. There was one sure way she could find out if she'd become repulsive to him.

She reached out and touched his knee, then slid her hand slowly up the inside of his leg. In a soft voice, she said, "Just because I can't, Tim, doesn't mean you have to be deprived."

Before her hand reached his crotch, he stepped back, away from her.

Her heart hurt. Louder than any words, that he would put himself out of her reach must be a statement of how he felt.

Tim cleared his throat, stalling for time. He was tempted by her offer, but if *she* couldn't, *he* wouldn't. It wasn't fair. Judging from her responses in the past, when she touched him with hands or lips, she became highly aroused—which he loved, of course. But since release was forbidden her, he couldn't let her sacrifice herself.

"It's not necessary, Lindsay. Really. I don't want you to do that."

And then, in case he weakened, he made an excuse to leave the room.

When she was alone, Lindsay crossed her arms over her swollen breasts and hugged herself in misery. Oh, God! she thought. *I'm so ugly to him that he doesn't want me anymore.*

She tried to console herself that the day would come when, after the babies were born, she would have her old body back—the body Tim had loved and desired. But *would* she? She'd exercise, of course, but forty-year-old bodies simply weren't as resilient as the twenty-year-old one she'd had when she bore Dina. The idea that Tim might never again want her as he'd once wanted her was too appalling to consider. She shut her eyes to it and tried very hard to concentrate on the babies. That was her job, now; keeping them safe.

TIM HAD BEEN WRONG when he said he could handle everything at home and at work, Lindsay thought, three weeks later. Not without killing himself or, at best, making himself ill from overwork.

He must think he was Superman. No one could do as much as he was doing. He came home from the office every day to fix lunch for her—and wouldn't listen when she suggested they hire someone to do that—and rushed home as early every afternoon as he could.

Almost every day, he brought her something—a frilly bed jacket, an African violet in a pretty pot, a book he thought she'd like. And buying those thoughtful little items must use some of his valuable time, too; he simply wasn't the kind to send an employee on a personal errand.

The late-afternoon and evening hours, he devoted to entertaining her with jokes and stories about what was happening in the office. It was as if he'd set himself the task of being amusing, as if he were on stage—except when he left her for a while to prepare dinner, as he was doing now.

But how *much* he was doing for her, Lindsay had only discovered a few nights ago. She'd awakened needing to use the loathsome bedpan and had found Tim's half of the bed empty. Questioning him the next morning, she'd finally pried out of him the admission that he was getting up by four or five every morning to do work he'd brought home with him from the office.

Her work. Someone had had to take up the slack, and naturally it had been Tim.

Unfortunately Dr. Mercador had seconded Tim's forbidding her to try to work in bed. "You'd end up twisting around, trying to reach this and that. I want you lying still, lady. And don't you forget it."

She *couldn't* forget it. Not for a minute was it out of her mind that her children's lives were at stake.

But, oh, Lordy, what a toll it was taking on Tim. Bit by bit, during the last week or so, she'd seen his face grow haggard and his eyelids darken until they looked bruised.

And it was her fault.

If Tim had married someone younger...

If she hadn't let herself get pregnant...

If. If. No matter how she looked at it, she was to blame.

A WEEK LATER, seated behind his desk, Tim put his head in his hands and let his eyes close for a moment. He was so damned tired. He hadn't told Lindsay that one of the reasons he'd had to bring work home almost every night was that Jack Bartlett had quit to move to a larger firm. He'd finally hired a replacement for Jack, but in the meantime, he'd also taken on four new regular accounts. With the twins on the way, it seemed important to him that the partnership's financial base be solid.

Lindsay had been after him to hire someone to replace her—not that anyone *could* replace her—and it was now evident that he had no other option.

He picked up the phone and dialed Harry Galla-gher, a friend who taught accounting at a nearby university. Harry always had a list of employable people. After the mandatory small talk, Tim asked, "Do you know any qualified CPAs who'd like to have about four months of steady work?"

"I might. I'll make a few calls and let you know."

After he'd hung up, Tim thought of calling Harry back and telling him that the job might last longer than that.

Their original decision had been that Lindsay would stay home for the first couple of months after their children were born, so she could nurse the babies during their all-important first weeks of life. But she'd planned to return to work as soon as possible after that. They'd even checked out day-care facilities in the neighborhood.

But then, later, Lindsay had said it might be better to find a trustworthy individual who would come into their home. So, they'd never really solidified their plans.

For all he knew, she'd changed her mind and decided to stay away from work longer. And recently, although he'd tried, he couldn't get her to talk much about what they should do.

For that matter, he couldn't get Lindsay to talk much at all, lately. She said it was because, stuck in the house, she didn't have anything to talk about. But Tim thought it was more than that. She seemed to have withdrawn from him; and her silences were the mark of a gap that, every day, he felt was widening between them.

And she would hardly let him touch her. It was ages since she'd let him smooth her skin with lotion. He understood, or tried to. His touching must arouse her— Lord knew, it aroused him plenty—and it was natural that she wouldn't want, now, to be aroused. Her withdrawal, too, he supposed was natural.

He'd tried to allow for that. And even though he missed her all day and longed for the time he could spend with her, he'd deliberately started giving her a little more space. He stayed downstairs a little longer when he went to clean up the kitchen after preparing a meal. And last night, experimentally, he hadn't returned upstairs after dinner for a couple of hours. Lindsay hadn't complained about it; obviously she didn't care, didn't miss him.

It was because she was pregnant, he told himself. But, damn it all, he was lonely for her—for her touch, for their old, easy flow of conversation. The only consolation was that at night, when he was certain she was asleep, he could put his hand on her hair or her arm, or slide his thigh against hers, and feel some faint echoes of their old communion.

"WELL, Ms. PATTERSON, I think I can give you about a ninety-percent assurance that the job is yours," Tim said. Harry had come up with a winner. Rona Patterson was a bright, ambitious young woman who was candid about seeking experience in a small firm because she meant one day to start one of her own.

"What'll it take to get the other ten percent?" She sounded wary and he realized, that, as an attractive young woman, she must fear there could be strings attached.

Knowing that what he was about to say would allay Ms. Patterson's fears, Tim grinned. He had decided that Lindsay deserved a chance to approve or disapprove of the woman who would occupy her office for the next several months.

"Before I hire you, I'd like it if you'd come home with me and meet my wife."

Ms. Patterson smiled broadly. "Sure. That's no problem at all."

WITH A COMB in one hand, a small hand-mirror in the other, Lindsay gazed critically at herself. It was one thing to receive friends who called—Joanne being a regular and faithful visitor—but quite another to have a stranger visit. Tim had telephoned a few minutes before to say he was bringing home a possible temporary replacement for Lindsay at work, but that before he hired the woman, he wanted Lindsay to meet her and tell him what she thought.

What she thought, primarily, was that she was glad Tim had given in and decided to hire someone to fill the gap left by her absence.

What she *felt*, though, was awful. It shouldn't have to be this way. She should have been able to work alongside Tim nearly until the birth; it wasn't as if their job entailed throwing heavy crates around, after all.

She'd let him down. It wasn't her fault, not exactly; her *body* had let her down, or it could safely have carried the twins.

Her *old* body, she thought darkly.

And the mirror did not give her an encouraging picture. Her hair had lost its sheen; her face was puffy; the dark shadows beneath her eyes seemed to have become permanent fixtures on her face.

She gave a last impatient tug of the comb through her hair, then thrust it and mirror into the top drawer of the nightstand as she heard the front door open, then close, and voices start to float up the stairs.

"I'm very happy to meet you, Ms. Patterson," Lindsay said, extending her hand a few moments later.

"Please call me Rona," said the slim, young blond woman, taking Lindsay's hand. "I feel as if I know you already. Your husband has told me so much about you."

"Oh, has he?" Lindsay murmured vaguely. It was all she could do to force herself to make eye contact with Rona Patterson. Though on the phone, Tim had told her about the woman's qualifications, he hadn't mentioned that she was a beauty. Thick blond hair fell past her shoulders, curling at the ends. Wide cornflower-blue eyes regarded Lindsay gravely as Ms. Patterson said how sorry she was that Mrs. Reynolds was having to spend all this time in bed.

Tim stood in the doorway. "I'll leave you two to get acquainted," he said. "I've invited Rona to stay for dinner."

"Oh, that's nice," Lindsay replied insincerely.

The worst of it, she thought later, when dinner was over, was that she couldn't bring herself to dislike Rona Patterson. She was competent as well as pleasant. She would be a genuine addition to the firm.

But at the moment, she was being an addition to the kitchen, Lindsay thought dismally. Rona Patterson had insisted on carrying down one of the dinner trays Tim had brought upstairs, and she had stayed down to help Tim with the after-supper chores. If Lindsay strained her ears very hard, she could hear their muted voices down there, talking as they worked.

And then, loud and clear, she heard a gust of Tim's unmistakable hearty laughter.

The sound hurt, for she realized how long it had been since *she'd* made Tim laugh like that. She couldn't entirely rid herself of the notion that Tim would have been much better off married to someone like Rona Patterson.

IT SEEMED LIKE AGES before she heard the front door close, then Tim's footsteps bounding up the stairs. He came into the room, smiling. Already, before Rona Patterson had done a lick of work, he looked less exhausted. "Well, what do you think? Will she do?"

"I think," Lindsay said dryly, "that she's absolutely *perfect.*"

11

TIM LAY PROPPED UP against the pillows beside Lindsay, his hands locked behind his head. He was talking about one of the new accounts he'd taken on since Lindsay's absence from the office had begun. "So, Van Struthers comes in with his tax returns for the past seven years. He's worried about an audit, because his brother-in-law just got nailed. And I swear, Lindsay, you've never seen such a mess. His accountant had missed half a dozen big deductions and claimed half a dozen others that look really fishy to me."

"Oh? Who was the accountant? Anybody we know?" It was an effort for her to put much interest into her voice. She felt so disconnected from the office these days. And also, inevitably, Tim's stories would include mention of Rona Patterson.

This one included her, too. Tim said, "No. But Rona knows him. She says . . ."

Lindsay stopped hearing. She *wasn't* jealous, she told herself fiercely. Not of Rona Patterson as an individual. It wasn't *her* fault that she'd taken Lindsay's place. And despite Tim's frequent mentions of Rona, Lindsay knew better than to think that he would ever be disloyal, in thought or deed.

But still, Rona Patterson was where *she* would have been, *should* have been. . . .

Tim had apparently said something funny—funny enough that he'd made himself laugh. But he cut off his chuckle, frowning as he stared at Lindsay. "Something wrong, love?"

She sighed. "I guess I'd just rather not hear about the office these days, Tim." She made a circle in the air with her hand. "It just . . . seems so far away. Nothing to do with me anymore."

"I'm sorry," Tim said slowly. "I just thought you'd like to be kept up-to-date."

Her guilt and frustration burst out of her as anger. "Well, I wouldn't. Okay?" she snapped.

He pulled back, increasing the distance between them. "*Okay!*"

What the hell *was* he going to talk to her about? he wondered. They'd wrapped up the question of the babies' names, choosing Katherine Anne for the girl, Clay Timothy for the boy. If Tim had still played racquetball each week, he could have described his games—sure to be enthralling for her, he thought dryly.

After a while, he said mildly, "There's one thing about the office we do need to discuss, Lindsay, and then I swear I'll never mention it again. But we've got to discuss what you're going to do about your going back to work after the twins are born."

"What's to discuss?" she asked dully. "Didn't we decide that already?"

Tim's eyebrows lifted. "Did we? I know we discussed it early on, but that was before we knew it was twins."

"So? I'm still planning to be back at work by March." At least she'd be able to help with *part* of the tax season, she thought.

"We hadn't talked about it in so long, I thought maybe you'd changed your mind."

Lindsay slid him a glance from the corner of her eye. Did he *want* her to change her mind and stay at home longer—or forever? Maybe he liked being in sole charge. But it was her business, too. In fact, she'd started it, bringing Tim in later to a firm that was already doing fairly well. "Well, I haven't changed my mind," she said coldly.

Tim counted to ten, then twenty. He'd done nothing to deserve that tone, he reflected. When he'd swallowed the worst of his hurt and annoyance, he suggested, "Then maybe I'd better start checking out some of those day-care places we looked into."

Her eyes widened. She'd told him. Or had she? Her days were so much the same, they blurred. Things she thought became indistinguishable from things she'd actually said. "I've got a woman who'll come to the house five days a week. Joanne found her for me. She's very nice—a grandmotherly type who loves babies and is just delighted to have something to do."

His voice had an edge to it. "I would have liked to be consulted on this, Lindsay."

The easy tears of pregnancy sprang to her eyes, but she refused to let her weakness show in her voice. "You have enough to do. I thought this was one thing *I* could handle."

Tim bit down hard on his lower lip. Okay, he could see her point. But still, it would have been something they could have done together, a small bridging of the gulf between them that seemed to widen every day.

He stole an oblique glance at her face. It was set, almost hard. He looked away again too quickly to notice the shininess of moisture in her eyes. What he saw was a woman who was shutting him out; an angry woman, a woman permeated by a deep unhappiness.

Loving her, he'd intended to do everything—anything—to make her happy, to fill her days and nights with joy.

You've done a damn fine job of it, haven't you, Tim?

SEATED AT THE SIDE of Lindsay's bed, Joanne grimaced. "And then, after putting up with all that pomposity—honestly, Lindsay, you should have seen the looks he gave me whenever I started to have a little fun!—at the end of the evening, he turned into an octopus."

"It sounds terrible," Lindsay said sympathetically.

"Oh, it was." Joanne cocked her head to one side. "You know, really, Lindsay, when you think about it, you don't have it so bad. I mean, I know it must be horrible having to lie in bed all the time, but in a few weeks the twins will be born, and you'll be able to resume a normal life. Well, as normal as it can be with two tiny babies. And you'll still have Tim." She wrinkled her nose. "And I'll still be dating disgusting bankers."

Lindsay barely heard Joanne's last remark. She wasn't so sure, she thought bleakly, that she had Tim anymore. Oh, he was dutiful. Several times a week, he brought her a present. And he still made an effort to converse with her, although with the office off-limits as a topic, he didn't have anywhere nearly as much to say.

And she was *cared for*—with meals and clean sheets and freshly laundered nightgowns. She couldn't fault a thing. He was absolutely wonderful to her.

Except it didn't seem as if he was really there anymore.

And why should he be? she wondered. What was he getting in return for all the care he lavished on her? A partner who was a liability instead of an asset; a wife who couldn't do a thing to help; a lover—

Not a lover. She couldn't think how long it had been since he'd touched her or encouraged her to touch him. Since the day when she'd seen him look away from her distended body, and then, a moment later, he'd refused to let her touch him, she hadn't dared make the slightest move toward physical contact, for fear of being rebuffed.

And the silences between them grew longer and longer, Tim's absences from her room after dinner each night lengthier.

She blinked, realizing from the fact that Joanne was looking at her oddly that her current silence must have stretched on too long.

"Sorry, Joanne. I was thinking . . ."

"Obviously," Joanne said dryly.

". . . about your problem," Lindsay lied. "This may sound like a silly question, but if bankers are so awful, why do you keep going out with them?"

"Because the only men I meet are the ones who are active in the charitable stuff I do. They aren't all bankers, but they might as well be. Bankers, lawyers, CEOs." She sighed. "What I wouldn't give to meet an Indian chief! At least he'd be different." She giggled wickedly. "If he said 'How!' I'd say—" her voice changed to a low, seductive purr "—'Any way you want.'"

Lindsay couldn't help being cheered up by Joanne. She had to smile. "Joanne, that's *terrible!*"

"I know," Joanne agreed cheerfully. "And besides, I don't think Indians really do say 'How,' except in awful old movies." She gave Lindsay an outrageous wink. "But I'd sure be willing to find out."

"TIM?"

Tim looked up in surprise at the sound of Nancy Buttrick's voice. The secretary stood just inside the door of his office, "Sorry," she said. "You mustn't have heard me knock."

"It's all right, Nancy." He paused. "Need me for something?"

"I just wondered if you wanted me to lock up. It's way past quitting time, boss."

"Is it?" Tim said vaguely. He had been sitting, thinking about the way things were nowadays between him and Lindsay. His wife—the woman he loved, the woman who was bearing his children—had become a stranger, and he didn't know what to do about it.

"Something wrong, boss?" Nancy asked with concern.

He shook his head. "No. Everything's fine. You run along. I'll lock up." He stood and tried to smile. "See you tomorrow."

A FEW WEEKS LATER, Lindsay lay in bed, trying to lighten the intensity of her despair with the thought that it was almost over. Dr. Mercador, when she'd last seen him three days before, had said that the twins might be born any day now.

And that visit to the doctor had been in itself a kind miracle. He'd decreed that she was far enough along to come to his office; it wouldn't matter, now, if moving around *did* bring on labor.

With the wonder of a convict coming out from behind bars from the first time in years, she had sat in the passenger seat while Tim drove, and stared hungrily at ordinary houses, ordinary shops, ordinary people doing ordinary things.

She had tried, hesitantly, to convey something of what she felt to Tim, but he had seemed too distant for her to share with him these tremulous feelings of freedom after having been caged. His remoteness and the fact that she couldn't tell him how she felt had doused her excitement, like a bucket of water poured over a tiny, flickering flame.

Even the fact that she was allowed now to move a little around the house brought her no real enjoyment. She was so heavy, so unbalanced, and so weak from nearly three months in bed that she hardly dared to walk unless Tim was right at her side. And having Tim beside her was no longer the joy it once would have been, but a torment.

She shifted restlessly. She'd been having Braxton Hicks contractions—otherwise known as false labor—all day. Nothing new, really. She'd been having them for weeks, and they hadn't settled into any pattern indicative of labor.

And she had a hunch her discomfort was more mental than physical, anyway. During the last few days, all the unhappy thoughts she'd had had begun to weave themselves into a design whose message was unmistakable: Tim didn't love her anymore.

He'd realized what a mistake he'd made in marrying her. But being the honorable, good man he was, he'd never admit the truth while she was pregnant. Therefore it was the strain of trying to pretend that kept him so distant, so grim-faced, so tormented looking.

Furthermore, being the kind of man he was, he might *never* tell her how he really felt.

That being the case, she had no choice; she had to set him free.

Having reached her decision, Lindsay decided to act on it as soon as possible. Maybe acting, however painful it was, would relieve the unbearable restlessness she felt.

At that moment, she heard Tim come in the front door. To keep him from veering off to the kitchen or the family room, as he often did these days instead of coming straight upstairs, she called his name.

He appeared in the doorway. If his smile had had even a trace of its old warmth, she might have been undone. But although he pulled his lips back, the smile he gave her was grim and strained.

Heartbroken, she steeled herself for what she had to do.

"How are you doing?" he asked.

She gestured to the chair beside the bed. "Sit down, Tim. I think we'd better talk."

She hadn't rehearsed this speech at all, but she knew instinctively that if she told him the plain truth—that she knew he'd realized she was the wrong person to be his wife—he'd simply deny it.

Tim sat down on the edge of the chair, and she began slowly, "Lying here in bed day after day, I've had plenty of time to think. I'm afraid what I've been thinking isn't very pleasant, but it has to be said."

He said nothing, only sat there.

"I don't think it'll come as much of a surprise to you if I say that I think this marriage was a mistake." She inhaled sharply as a particularly strong Braxton Hicks contraction gripped her. Or *was* it a Braxton Hicks? Hadn't there been several like that one in the past few hours, at steadily decreasing intervals?

Tim's expression turned to one of anxiety. "Are you all right, Lindsay?"

She waved a hand. "I'm fine. It's nothing. Let me go on, Tim. It's my fault, you see. I think what happened was that you caught me right in the middle of a little old midlife crisis. Somewhere deep inside, without knowing that was what I wanted, I must have hungered to have another child. Women do, as they approach the end of their childbearing years, you know."

Another contraction hit her. *Not* a Braxton Hicks. Maybe none of them today had been Braxton Hickses, and she'd been too preoccupied to realize it. She said hurriedly, "But blaming nature is no excuse, Tim. I did wrong—to both of us—when I maneuvered you into getting me pregnant. And I multiplied that wrong by marrying you."

Tim's face was granite and when he spoke, his voice was like a knife. "You're saying you *used* me? That you never loved me at all?"

She couldn't say she didn't love him. That was too much of a lie.

"I *did* use you, Tim," she said, skirting the lie. "And I'm terribly sorry for it." Another grinding pain made her bite her lip. "But just because we made a mistake doesn't mean we have to pay for it the rest of our lives. As soon as the babies come, I think we should separate."

She managed to shift her attention from what was going on inside her body to focus briefly on his face. She saw him nod slowly, as if the movement was painful to him. "If that's what you want."

She let out a giggle that sounded crazy and probably was. "You won't have to stick around for very long. I—" She broke off as she felt an internal rupturing and a gush of wetness flooded out of her.

He was standing, leaning over her, staring intently at her face. "What is it, Lindsay?"

"My water," she explained, gesturing helplessly downward at the soaked bed.

His face changed. For a moment, he looked at her the way he used to, back when she thought he loved her. His eyes were dark with emotion. Then his face went blank, as if an unseen hand had wiped across it. He nodded once, brusquely. "I'd better call the doctor right away...."

THE HOSPITAL waiting room was the same one where Tim had waited the night miscarriage had threatened the twins. He had thought, until now, that that night was the worst he'd ever experienced. But the fear, that night, had been mixed with hope. *This* night was far, far worse in its heavy and utter hopelessness.

The things Lindsay had said to him were bad enough—confirmation of his own unhappy thoughts about their marriage. And if he'd had any reason to disbelieve her, that reason would have flown an hour before when, after checking her into the hospital, he'd automatically started to go with her to her room and she'd told him no. She'd rather be alone in labor, than with him.

The only difference in the way the two of them viewed the situation was that she seemed to think it was her fault, while he knew it was his.

He had overwhelmed her with his love, seduced her into an affair, deliberately gotten her pregnant, and coerced her into marrying him.

It had been him, wanting what *he* wanted, taking what he wanted, thinking that how much he loved her was all that mattered. And now that he knew what a selfish monster he'd been, how could he refuse to let her go?

He put his head in his hands and his shoulders shook as tears filled his eyes and ran down his cheeks.

LINDSAY PANTED like a dog lying in the hot summer sun.

That last contraction had been longer, more intense.

An understatement. It had been all-consuming, gripping her in an iron fist of pain.

The nurse, who had been in and out of her room, had murmured the not-particularly-helpful information that she was entering transition—the last stage before the babies actually began to make their way down the birth canal.

Now the nurse leaned over her. "You're coming along nicely, dear."

If this was "nicely," Lindsay wondered, then what on earth was it like when it wasn't so "nice"...? The thought trailed away as a new contraction began to build. Her open eyes stared straight at the lines pleating the gray-haired nurse's forehead. If only it were Tim's face over her, his hand holding hers. She'd sent him away because she'd thought she couldn't bear to look at him, knowing it was over....

"Are you sure you wouldn't like your husband to be with you, dear? I saw him out in the waiting room a little while ago. The poor thing looks quite upset," said the worried-looking nurse.

Another wave began to roll toward her—already. She wasn't prepared. She hadn't even stabilized her breathing. Her mouth opened and words she hadn't known she was going to say burst out of her: "Yes, yes! I want him. *Tim!*"

HIS MISERY was inducing hallucinations, Tim guessed. He thought he'd heard Lindsay's voice calling his name, from very far away. But still . . .

A nurse appeared in the doorway—an older woman with frizzy gray hair. Heedless of the tears on his cheeks, he leaped up and rushed toward her.

A LITTLE OVER AN HOUR later, Tim was back in the waiting room, in the same chair he'd occupied before. But it was a different man who sat there now.

He was back out here, instead of with his wife, because Lindsay was being prepped for a cesarean delivery. Dr. Mercador had arrived and, after examining Lindsay, had decided that things were moving too slowly for the well-being of mother and children.

"We often end up doing a C-section with twins," the obstetrician had said.

But even so, the bleak hopelessness Tim had felt before was gone. Something here wasn't adding up. The bottom line wasn't totaling out as it should. The way Lindsay had looked at his face, the way she'd held his hand, hadn't jibed with the image of a woman who professed not to love him, who insisted she had only used him to achieve motherhood.

Had she lied with that whole spiel she'd given him a few hours back?

If so, why?

He had a little time, now, to think it out. And he meant to use every minute of it.

12

LINDSAY AWOKE SLOWLY from what felt as if it had been a brief doze. Her private room was cheerful, the yellow walls bordered top and bottom with a design of stylized orange daisies. A window at the left of her bed showed a square of pale blue early-December sky.

Despite her nap, she was permeated by exhaustion. The twins were in the nursery now, although later, they would spend most of the time, except at night, in the room with her, in rolling cots.

Tim had been with her for the birth and immediately afterward. He hadn't said much, just held her hand. But he wasn't here now; he must have gone somewhere while she slept.

Get used to it, Lindsay, she thought. Though she was certain he would become and remain a part of the twins' lives—and she certainly wouldn't hinder his fathering—he wouldn't be an integral part of *her* life anymore. Custody arrangements... They'd have to talk about that.

But she couldn't think about it now; she needed to close her eyes again. Her last sight, before her lashes drifted downward, was of the IV tube connected with her left arm and leading up to the bag of clear liquid on its rolling stand.

SHE AWAKENED AGAIN at the sound of the door opening. Even though she kept her eyes closed, she knew that the person entering was Tim. It was *his* presence, not a doctor or a nurse, that she felt nearby. She could also feel that something was going to burst out of him. And she wouldn't be able to handle it. She had no strength left to do battle with Tim, if indeed it was the rage for battle she felt emanating from him.

Slowly her lashes lifted and she saw him seating himself only inches from the bed. His expression was implacable. The eyebrows that she could usually read as an accurate barometer of his feelings were dead level, unrevealing.

His voice, though soft, was resolute. "Don't say anything, Lindsay. I know you're worn-out, and for most of this you won't have to do a whole lot of talking. First of all..." He inhaled deeply; his voice gentled. "First of all, Katie and Clay are absolutely beautiful. You did a magnificent job, Lindsay."

"I didn't—"

He silenced her with a fingertip pressed to her lips. "Hush. This isn't the part where you have to talk. Not yet. Actually, I could go on for days about those two and how I feel about them. And I probably will, once those babies' mom and dad get a few things settled."

Her mouth opened. He said fiercely, "I told you to hush! You got to do a lot of talking last night. Now it's my turn." He settled himself back in the chair. "Now, the second point... I debated with myself long and hard about having this conversation with you now, so soon after your ordeal. 'It wouldn't be fair to Lindsay,' I said to myself. 'Wait until she's in better condition.'" A bitter noise erupted from his lips. "And then I realized how funny those scruples were. We're talking life-and-death here, Lindsay. *My* life. *Your* life. The life of those babies. And I'm worrying about being *fair*? Forget it!"

He leaned forward, fixing her with his gaze. "So, have you figured out the main topic of this conversation yet, Lindsay? I hope so, because I'm going to cut right to the point. Now you get to speak, if you've got an answer. When did you stop loving me?"

"I—"

"Come on. Tell me. What day did it happen? What hour? Or if you don't remember, at least describe the occasion, the reason, the..."

She had no strength; she'd known that from the beginning. And that meant that she lacked the energy to lie. "I...I didn't," she said weakly. "I didn't stop loving you."

He folded his arms across his chest. "I thought not. You didn't act as if you didn't love me last night, when I was holding your hand and you were screaming out my name."

She lowered her gaze and the room blurred as she tried to see through the tears that clung to her lashes. "All right. So you know that," she admitted in a voice that was little more than a thread of sound. "But it doesn't have to matter, Tim. I don't want to hold you— you don't have to stay with me. I'm a grown-up. I'll survive."

"Sure, you will. I have no doubt about that. You're a strong lady." There was a little color in his voice. Not warmth, but at least it was no longer the flat, dead thing it had been before. And now it took on new fervor. "But why in the name of God should you have to? If you love me, why are you trying to get rid of me?"

She turned her head to see him rising, looming over her. He took her shoulders in his hands and, looking as if he'd like to shake her battered body, instead demanded, "Why, Lindsay, why? It doesn't make a lick of sense."

"Because . . . because . . ."

"Because what? Why? You've *got* to tell me!"

The words whipped out of her, propelled by their own force. "Because *you* don't love *me* anymore."

"What?" His hands came away from her as he rocked back on his heels, as if she'd struck him a physical blow.

"Please don't try to deny it, Tim," she implored him. "A blind woman could have seen it. And who could blame you? I wouldn't have been able to love me, either—a big lump, lying there, not able to do anything, not able to help—" her voice broke "—too old to even carry your children properly, the way a woman should—"

"Lindsay!" He cut her off. He was back in his chair, but leaning forward so his face was just above hers. "That's how you felt? Why didn't you tell me?"

"I couldn't. I felt so . . . guilty for getting pregnant and forcing you into marrying me."

"Guilty!" He stood, shoving his fingers through his hair. "Oh, Lord, Lindsay. That's how *I* felt. Guilty that I'd gotten you pregnant, feeling as if I'd forced my love on you. . . ."

"Guilty? *You?*"

He nodded. "Do you know what we did, Lindsay? Me as much as you. Do you remember that pretty speech I made when we first got together—about how if we were honest with each other, everything would be all right?"

She nodded.

"Well, I was absolutely right when I said all that." He grimaced. "I could pat myself on the back for being right, I suppose. But then, I'd need to administer a good

swift kick where it hurts the most—for *not doing it.*
And I didn't make *you* do it, either. I—" He cut himself
off and eased himself down so he was seated on the side
of the bed. "We can fix it. I know we can. But we'll have
to be careful. It's so easy *not* to say the things that need
to be said. I just found that out, because I almost forgot to say the most important thing of all."

His hand was on her, wrapped around her forearm
just above her elbow, and she felt the warmth of the old
connection flowing through her as he said, "I never
stopped loving you, Lindsay. Not for a moment. I love
you now with all my heart. When I thought I was going
to lose you, I . . ." A shudder wracked his whole body.
"I'll be very careful, love, because I know you're hurting, but I absolutely *have* to hold you now."

Lindsay opened her free arm to him, in acceptance
and in welcome.

Slowly he eased himself down beside her on the bed.
One arm went around behind her; he buried his lips in
the curve of her throat. "Lindsay, my love," he said
huskily.

She clung to him, her one available hand pressing
deep into his back. She was aching with love, yet fear
still clung to her. Things had gone so terribly wrong
between them; how could they ever go back and make
it right?

It was as if Tim had read her mind. "We can do it,"
he assured her. "All we have to do is go back and say
all the things we didn't say."

Yes . . . she could see it happening, imagine it unfold-
ing between them. It would take time, but they would
have the time, now that she knew Tim loved her, and
he knew she loved him. That was the foundation; the
rest of the house could be rebuilt. She tightened her

hold on her love, her husband, her partner for life, and let herself sob out the pain.

She wasn't aware of anyone in the room until a shocked-sounding female voice exclaimed, "Mr. Reynolds! Mrs. Reynolds! Really, you shouldn't!"

Tim lifted his head for only an instant. "Oh, yes, we should." And then, heedless of the nurse, he kissed her.

"IT'S LIKE UNPEELING the layers of an onion, isn't it?" Lindsay suggested to Tim. Because of the cesarean, she'd had to stay in the hospital for three days; she and the twins were scheduled to go home day after tomorrow. Tim was with her constantly, the hospital having obligingly provided a cot so he could spend the night in her room.

Rona Patterson, with the help of the more experienced staff, was handling the office. And although Lindsay had never thought she'd enjoy hearing what a treasure Ms. Patterson was, now she was delighted, since it was her competence that let Tim be *here* instead of *there*. Come to think of it, though, Tim probably would just have shut down the office if he'd had to. He'd made it plain that unraveling the knots and tangles in their relationship was his most important task.

That and loving the twins, of course, who were in the nursery since it was after ten at night.

Tim was sitting beside Lindsay's bed, his fingers entwined with hers. He grinned as he looked closely at her face. "Something's hurting you, Lindsay. What is it?"

Even now, she couldn't look at him as she said, "That day, when you wouldn't let me touch you, when you first found out I couldn't...really make love. And right before that . . . you couldn't even look at me." She drew a deep breath. "I know I wasn't a very pretty sight, but . . ."

Tim's jaw dropped. "Not a pretty sight? Good heavens, Lindsay! You've always been absolutely beautiful to me." His brow furrowed. "I'm trying to think what could possibly have given you that impression. It was . . ." His face cleared. "That was too much love, not too little. I guess it was a trace of the old macho stuff getting in the way," he said. "I should have just told you how I felt."

And then it was his turn to confess how much it had hurt to feel her withdraw from him, and her turn to explain and apologize for all the mistakes and assumptions she'd made.

As they talked, Lindsay took Tim's hand and held on tightly. She knew they still had a lot of work to do, communicating all the things they should have communicated during those long, wracking months she had spent in bed; but they were together now, working together to demolish the wall they'd built.

"YOU LOOK RADIANT, lady!" Joanne pouted. "It's not fair that you should go through all that and look like you do!"

Lindsay smiled, aware that it was probably an irritatingly smug smile that curved her lips. "I'm feeling pretty good," she admitted in superficial words that cloaked her deep, inner happiness.

"Say, Dina seems to be taking to the twins like a duck to water," Joanne remarked brightly.

Joanne had arrived the day before when Dina was there, not only visiting her mother, but sitting in one of the easy chairs, holding a twin in each arm.

"I think it's really okay now," Lindsay said, holding up crossed fingers. "She actually volunteered to baby-sit Katie and Clay some weekend, once I've stopped nursing, so Tim and I can get away by ourselves."

"All *right!*" Joanne enthused.

"And," Lindsay continued, "she has a boyfriend. Gary. From the sound of it, he's a really nice kid. She's going to bring him home some weekend soon and Mom'll *really* be able to check him out."

They went on talking for a while longer. Then Joanne rose, blowing kisses to the angelic-looking infants asleep in their wheeled cots. She paused on her way to the door. "Oh, shoot! Those kids are so cute, *I* might even baby-sit for you, if you get desperate."

Lindsay's eyes rounded. "Good Lord! What a sacrifice!"

"And don't you forget it! Oh, hi, Tim," Joanne said as the door opened and Lindsay's husband entered the room. He kissed Joanne's cheek, then came over and bestowed a more intimate kiss on his wife. He smiled down at her lovingly, but then, as if pulled by a magnet, went over to gaze tenderly at his children.

Lindsay's heart turned over with love as she observed him.

Joanne looked from Lindsay to Tim and back again. "Well, I was just on my way out, folks. Bye."

"Bye, Joanne."

Tim seemed reluctant to pull his gaze from the twins. Then, with a big smile, he sat down in the easy chair. "I *love* being a daddy," he announced unnecessarily. "Especially since you're the mommy, love."

She was going to be a working mommy. One of the things she had recently learned about herself was that her work was essential to her well-being, so she and Tim had decided she would resume an active role in the firm almost at once. An hour or two a day, at first, with the twins in bassinets beside her desk. Later, as she felt ready, she'd increase her time and commitment. Tim was all for it, pointing out that that way, he would have his whole family with him at work.

"Doting" was far too mild a description for how Tim felt, she thought, seeing his eyebrows lower in disappointment as two nurses entered the room. "Already?" he complained.

The older of the two, a pretty black woman with a calm, professional manner that Lindsay especially liked, glanced meaningfully at the black-and-white schoolroom-style clock high on the wall opposite Lindsay's bed. "Ten o'clock," she pointed out. It was the hour when the babies were returned to the nursery for the night.

Lindsay sighed. She hated it as much as Tim did when the twins had to go. But she did enjoy their evening promenades, with all the other doting mothers and fathers, to the nursery to watch through the window as the babies were sorted out and settled down for the night.

Lindsay leaned on Tim's arm as they went down the hall, not so much because she still needed his physical support but because the contact with him felt so good, so right.

Halfway to the nursery, another couple came out of one of the rooms. The man—short, red-haired and freckle-faced—grinned a hello, echoed by a shyer smile from his tiny, brown-haired wife. "You're the parents with the twins, aren't you?" he asked.

"Yes," Lindsay replied. "We are."

She heard the happiness in her own voice and realized that the "we" feeling was back. Perhaps it had never really vanished, after all; it had just gotten buried by the debris of things left unsaid.

THE "WE" FEELING was still there when Lindsay and Tim got back to her room, and with that as an anchor and support, she was able to say, "There's one thing I haven't really talked about that I was feeling pretty strongly all those weeks in bed." She felt physically well enough, now that she was comfortable sitting up in one of the easy chairs. Tim had moved the other one around to sit in so their hands could brush or touch or cling as they talked. Their fingers were touching lightly now and the warm vein of connection seemed to Lindsay to be binding them together more strongly with each confession.

"Tell me now," he urged her.

"The age thing," she said bluntly. Tim looked about to speak, but she hurried on: "I feel as if I've tried to talk about it before—all through our relationship—and you've always brushed it aside. Maybe it shouldn't matter to me, but it does. When I was feeling awful, lying there with you having to do everything for me, I kept thinking it was because I was too old that this was happening to us."

This was an area where he'd really blown it, Tim decided. Because the difference in their ages seemed so unimportant to him, he'd never truly understood that to Lindsay, it loomed large and menacing.

He inscribed a vivid mental note in a file to be examined frequently throughout the years, that it might *always* bother her, and that he should *always* take the time to listen, to understand, to reassure....

"First of all," he told her, "when I look at you, I see a woman who is beautiful both inside and out, a woman who is the mother of my children, but even more than that, the love of my life." He paused, disentwined his fingers from hers to gently caress her cheek, then took her hand between both of his. "So, tell me, Lindsay. Tell me what worries you. Tell me all of it."

LINDSAY LOOKED AROUND the twins' room. The nightlight was on; two sweet pink babies lay sleeping soundly. *Perfect!*

She felt as if she might burst from excitement, not untinged with a little apprehension. She'd had her checkup today and the doctor had informed her that she was ready for complete physical sharing of her love for Tim.

Not, she thought with a wry grin, that they hadn't found some perfectly delightful means of sensual expression in the meantime.

She felt a hand on her shoulder. "All's right with the world, isn't it?" Tim's voice spoke quietly.

"Sure is," she breathed. She turned her head, tilting her chin up so she could look into his eyes. He knew. She knew. The locking of their gazes alone kindled her desire.

In a comical, almost furtive hurry, they tiptoed down the hall and into the big bedroom. The accoutrements of Lindsay's bedridden period were long gone, thoroughly cleared away by Tim before Lindsay and the twins came home from the hospital. All she really could see now, anyway, was the bed.

Moments later, she and Tim were on it, naked. Propped up on one arm, he lay on his side, caressing her. She had done some toning up since the birth, but her body wasn't back to normal yet. And there were stretch marks that would never go away—marks that Tim insisted were badges of honor.

Yet, even with those marks and some soft, spongy places she was determined to rid herself of eventually, Lindsay had no doubt, looking at her husband's rapt face, that she was beautiful to him.

He leaned over and kissed some of the spots he'd only touched with his hands so far this evening. Then, stretching out his body so it half covered hers, he kissed her deeply, passionately. His tongue invading her mouth in a presaging of the sexual act made her blood pound; her lower body felt heavy and hot with wanting.

She reached down and circled Tim's arousal with her hand. He was fully erect, as hard as ivory. "I want you . . . now," she said insistently. It seemed like a lifetime since she had felt him inside her, filling her, completing her, joining their bodies in the same way that they were once again joined in spirit.

He obliged. Birth control was no longer a problem since Tim had had a vasectomy. So when he entered her, it was with his naked self. The sensation was so exquisite that Lindsay let out a cry of rapture—a rapture that built to ecstasy as he moved in a steady crescendo, each stroke seeming deeper, more compelling than the one before.

He was a pace before her this time in achieving release, but as he groaned, her own pleasure exploded into pinwheels of delight. "I love you," she cried out.

"My love," he echoed, holding her as her paroxysms died.

Later, in his arms, with her head on his chest, she heard his voice rumble in her ear. There was a trace of amusement in his tone. "Anything you feel like saying?"

It had almost become a joke between them, this mutual insistence on sharing everything nowadays.

"I feel," Lindsay said with a smile, "that I adore you, mister."

"Only 'adore'?" He mimed disappointment. "I can do better than *that*—" He broke off as a whimper drifted down the hall, in the next instant turning into a full-blown squall.

Tim sighed. "Clay."

"At least he waited *long* enough," Lindsay reminded with a wink.

"True, true." A second cry joined the first. "Very thoughtful children you produced, I must admit."

"*I* produced?" Lindsay protested. "You had a hand in it, you know."

Tim's eyebrows bobbled wickedly. "I wouldn't have called it a 'hand,' exactly."

They got out of bed, pulling on robes. As they started toward the twins' room, Lindsay persisted. "Okay, what's better than 'adore'?"

He looped his arm around her shoulders and pulled her close against his side. "Later, love. There's no hurry. After all, we've got plenty of time."

"Yes, we do," Lindsay agreed as they entered the babies' room. *We've got the rest of our lives.*

Six exciting series for you every month... from Harlequin

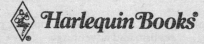